What to do when life pushes you to the edge, leaving you feeling cornered, scared, helpless? What to do when you feel abandoned, distressed, tired?

PROLOGUE

Life is fleeting.
To live or die is not the question.
The how-to could be, but not the when.

Those in need of saving might be ignored and those not in need of it could receive it.
For some, life could be as flimsy as the weather, and for others as the mind of mankind.
For some, they are pushed into the market called life unprotected.
For most, life could be like a walk in the rain.

Life is elusive.
What it means to me could be different from what it does you.

For those still on a walk in the rain, for the curious, for the alumni and for the culprits, this book's my gift to you.

A WALK IN THE RAIN

DEBBIE WALTERS

August 2013

This is how it starts.
Bothered by your thoughts, you began to cry – worried, scared, helpless – your emotions were a mess. you lay still on the sunbathed paved floor in the backyard while your thoughts alternate from blank to jumbled up, like it had a mind of its own.
The whooshes of the air, the rustlings of the orange tree and the overall silence this part of the house had to offer was enough reason to make it your favourite spot.
The tree provided shade, but you chose to lay on the bare floor two meters away from the garden. Far enough to reveal your healing scars to the sun, yet close enough to receive the tree's fallen leaves.

Your dog laid beside you as you watched the clouds.
you watched the clouds change form,
you watched them bring life to your eyes,
you watched them move on while you remained still, quiet, mute. You have spent your long break like this, in peace. Contrary to the beliefs of others, we knew you weren't brooding; it is after all quiet afternoons like this that make life worth living.

Mother was at work and your sisters were either asleep or watching some cartoon for the umpteenth time. You were the eldest of you three by a year and a half, and by seven years. Strangers sometimes call you and the

younger twins, and you sometimes felt the urge to gouge their eyes out to give them a closer look.
Twenty-three wishes. Twenty-three times you've wished her death. A painful one at that.

Until now, it has been but a gradual process – the wishes – a common entrée of wishing to have been the only child to an escalation with the passage of time.

Over and over again, you wished for everything and anything that would make her disappear from your life even if it meant you had to take matters into your hands and kill her. Diminutive in comparison to the thirst for your own demise. But all of that changed two months ago, you started to think differently.

We started to think differently.

A WALK IN THE RAIN

Father says unlike the rest out there, you have a roof over your head, an education better than he ever received, a healthy and complete family – its mom, its three daughters and, there is Father – 'all healthy and bouncing'. A weird choice of words on his part. But then again, as mostly left unsaid – once born, it is a given to live.

Mother says not to hate Father, his absence is all for the family's wellbeing. But what no one understands is that you never once asked for any of this, you never asked to have a beating heart, let alone cohabit with a family in which its head raises his fist like the sky would drop if he had the slightest bit of restraint. They say he in heaven sees and knows all, then why has he not sent forth a helping hand despite your cries and prayers. The day your infant cousin lost her life; we demurred, "why not ours". The day your parents made a comparison of your situation with 'those out there who die of poverty with every passing day', we coveted their end. Death is said to evade when one yearns for it, then chase when least expected. Do you perhaps fear the truth in it?

We have repeatedly said no matter where we are in life, death is highly welcome. How well do you believe us?

Only if...
Only if hell wasn't murky,
Only if it was as easy as films depict, to leave this fastidiousness behind us and put these thoughts into action – how delightful would that be.

A WALK IN THE RAIN

*Time as they say changes a lot. maybe with time it will me.
Maybe with time I will learn to leave this fastidiousness behind
me, Maybe with time I will come to realise my hell,
Maybe...*

These you have said and these we have heard.

*You remember the first time the thought awoke in you, the first
time we came into existence, the first time life made you give us
a purpose? We a day old, you 3500. All you did was spend
what was rightfully yours but those imposing eyes, scary as
they were impelled to 'tell nothing but the truth'. You rebelled.
That's what it must have been, a childish rebellion, or maybe
just a fat lie. But what does a dog terrified of its master do? –
bite or appease? The answer lies in how sensible the dog is, if
wise it would appease its master but if foolish it would bite. Y o
u have lived knowing better than to be the foolish, the moment
you bite is when our ideal death gets thrown out the window
and you on the streets.*

*Although terrified by his question, you chose to play smart.
You foolishly thought you neither bit nor appeased, you were
satisfied and hoped to get away with it, so you headed for the
car.*
*You, high on sugar, thought all was well and dandy but your
sober sister knew better. She looked at you with that all too
well-known pity in her eyes.*

*That look's sure to become a habit of hers before long you
thought in attempt to shrug off that unsettling feeling. The*

feeling that informed you what type of face that was, the feeling that brought images of events that have been, thus are preceded and succeeded by that look.
It is the same face she makes before and after you get 'rightfully punished'.

Father's demeanour all the way home was the only confirmation needed to torment you while informing you that your trick was a failure, to assure you of the dread that laid in waiting. That moment onwards, everything became dreadful – the appalling sight of your sister, the sound of your very own breathing, the rays of sunlight that made its way into the car, and even life itself – the mere awareness of your existence.

Up.
Down.
Left. Right.
there was nothing. Nothing to take your mind away from those wild, vivid and veracious images, of how your body will soon come to look like, that ran wild in your mind.

The gates opened and the car made its way into the compound, Father left the car and stormed off without saying a word expecting your 9-year-old legs to catch up, so you followed as fast as you could. Your sister upon entering the house scurried to the room to save herself from becoming your messenger of pain. You on the other hand remained immobile by the door, waiting for orders.

A WALK IN THE RAIN

WANDE!!! He yelled.
Mu wire wa!
Bring me the wire!

She had a maximum of ten seconds and you none, you knew what he expected of you.

On your knees, uniform on, bags where he ordered to leave it - anywhere that was appropriate – you left it by the foot of the dining table. He asked ONE LAST TIME what you did with the money you got from paternal grandmother. This time you said things as they were – you bought junk to share with your friends, friends that will tomorrow not notice your impendent bruises nor your swollen and Father-inflicted scars.

It didn't take long. After giving a run-through as to what bought what and who bought who, it began.

The first hit was a mistake, it was on the face and was sure to leave a one-night scar. Doing more and he would expose the skeleton in his cupboard.
You as a family would be showing the world that Father's once in a year visit generally presumed as filled with laughter, gifts and expensive outings is in fact a little representation of reality. A reality in which his visits are always celebrated by gracing his first child with a serpent tongue-like wire on regular basis.
He would be showing that the picture-perfect family he has worked so hard to build is nothing but 'a façade'. At least that

is what he would often say about others but himself. It is after all innocent until proven guilty.

No one, not even mom, has succeeded in convincing him as to why his disciplinarian principles make him the epitome of hypocrisy. She like always, on that day, in her attempt to spare herself from being yelled at for HINDERING NECESSARY ACTIONS, remained in the room despite hearing your pleas.

Ironically it was always 'mommy' that came out whenever the first hit landed, you always kept at it until you realised how helpless your situation was and force stop.
You pretend doll.

But no matter how hard you tried you still felt the pain. You felt the constant stings of the wire, you felt as the two separated lines left humps upon humps of scars on your back, legs and fingers. You felt helpless. Weak.

You were weak, weak against pain, and it seemed like Father thought you could take it like a doll, like a champ or maybe he wanted something else - the screams of a desperate child, of a child pushed to the edge - so he took it a step further. He increased the tempo giving you little to no time to think. He circled around and the hits became even more unpredictable giving you little to no idea as to where and when the next hit would land. And although the hits, most of the time, hit the dress-like uniform before your back, you still thought you knew what it felt like to be in hell; you could smell pain, you could hear screams, you thought you could see the devil, so you whispered words...

Those you believed would have made him stop,
those that should have made him stop,
but made him continue...

I'm sorry, ... am really sorry,
I won't do it again
please...

Your words were slurry, your body and mind were all over the place, your breathing inconsistent. As your cheeks throbbed, so did your behind. The wire he ordered your sister to bring graced your body in all places but the area your school uniform was unable to hide. He kept reminding to raise your uniform and each time you obeyed your fingers got struck. Those hurt the most.

Father hurled as he flogged. You lost the first battle against your tears, but you were far from bawling – that dog might have been the wiser to appease, but to do that it bellowed. That is not who you are nor is it who you ever will be.
The marks of the snake on your arms and legs are proof and evidence of a battle fairly well-fought.

Each had a space in the middle and two swollen vertical bars on the sides. Some laid on each other and formed a tic tac toe template – unfortunate spots that got hit more than once, parts of your body that no longer felt like yours, red parts that felt heavy and screamed pain when in contact with another surface.

Today those red parts have become a reminder of our root, of the connection we share. Red parts that have turned black, scars that have begun to blend in with your skin as we have come to with you. Then, the redness paid the pain no justice, the pain however paid the hate justice.

You hated this man so much you could kill him. The money was yours and you had every right to spend it! What do those people know wishing they lived your life, wishing to have a Father like yours, wishing to receive new clothes from Germany, France, Italy..., wishing to share facial traits with their Fathers like you do yours. What do they know?

Anyone who saw your sister would be under the impression that she was the one undergoing torture. She looked miserable but seeing her comforted you.

Since the beginning she sat crouched on the rug at the very end of the living room, covering her ears to block out the whips we could hear ever so clearly, to block out the reality of the desperate coughs and tears you let out, to block out the thoughts we would have had if she was in your situation.

Despite the headaches you had from the constant and sudden movements your body made, you could still think. You could still see. You could still feel. We could think of the horrible things we would have done to this man if our roles were reversed, if he was in your situation but even more substantial was if Wande was in your situation.

We could clearly see no hesitation in his movements, in his words, in his insults. WE could clearly feel how desperate you were to stop feeling, to stop seeing, to stop thinking, to stop breathing. We felt all of it.

Mother knew better than to come out of her room whenever Father was in his 'trance' as we call it, but even more importantly she had to protect the youngest and save her from experiencing this ridiculous display of authority.

Around you were objects that represented happy memories, eidetic memories of how you and father scared Wande the day you got your dog, memories of trying out similar clothes Father bought for you two, memories of celebrating Father obtaining his permanent residence permit in Italy, lost memories that can only be seen in pictures of a period long gone. Memories of coming back from school just to smell Father's perfume and hear SURPRISE!! two seconds later. They became moments of false happiness.

You pondered on how it was possible for the person responsible for the only stable happiness in your life – Yankee – to be the same person responsible for persistently making your life miserable.

You were fed up. Exhausted.
Your nose kept running and Yankee was still barking - she was the loudest whenever a loud yell managed to slip out.

Some time passed, and the deed was done. You felt different and surely looked different, your face was a mess, now worse than your sister's, your skin felt like it was on fire and was soon about to feel worse. He ordered to bathe.

Your hate has now come to surpass the pain you feel, but acceptance is all that lays dormant at the end of it all. You will receive neither an apology nor comfort from those guilty of your situation. In its stead you received a lecture directed at you two doors away - 'I give them food, shelter, education, what more can they ask for'. A sentence meant to save them from the convictions yet to come.

Who is to blame for the tremendous pain you have come to suffer? All the painful experiences you have and will come to undergo just because you exist. We blame them for all of it and no one is to convince you otherwise.

Who wants an unrequested life? Most experiences call for endurance, that much is fact to you, but having to tolerate discomfort not from outsiders but from those that call you one of theirs is another story.

The established fact however is that mutiny is not for children, the healing reds and blending blacks on your body are enough to tell you that much.

Now. Tell us e x a c t l y what you want.

A WALK IN THE RAIN

Eyes closed, the last stream of tears flowed down both outer edges of my eyes, making their way to the already wet bedsheet. And although my nostrils were filled with the stench of my urine, I couldn't be less bothered.

Immobile on my bed, spaced out safe in my mind, dry, comfortable, and justifiably alone as my sister already fled to Mother's room, I stared at the ceiling fan as it rolled, following its slow movements, mimicking its tempo with my breathing until it became a subconscious action. Calm, I got off the bed pulled the sheets to the ground and slowly began to take off my wet pyjamas. Mother said to thoroughly clean up and ask the housekeeper for help, but I never did.

Done putting on a petticoat, I went to the bathroom, picked up a half-filled bag of detergent and two wash bowls. Before heading for the backyard, I went back to the room to check the time - there was some time left before breakfast.

With the soap in the laundry bin and the bin in the bowls, I continued with the process. First I passed the living room, ignoring the remnants of Father's visit that were proudly displayed on the rug – clothes, electronics and others, then climbed up the stairs that first led to the kitchen before the backyard. Two steps away from my destination, I paused, giving the housekeeper a second's glance before opening the locked back door.

The kitchen smelt of eggs, the scrambled ones.

The housekeeper went on with her day in the kitchen and paid me no attention, so neither did I her. Yankee on the other hand ran to greet me upon hearing the door open. I ruffled her fur and gave her a tummy rub before she satisfactorily took off for her morning ritual and left me with mine.

As I stomped on the soapy sheets in the wash bowl, I watched her run through the garden chasing lizards, hopping over the oranges and tangerines – both ripe and rotten – that stood in her path. Seeing her happily go on with her day brought a smile to my face, it always did.

Ever since she was a puppy Yankee enjoyed running in the compound, and before long I took on the habit of chasing and being chased by her. I thought of it as the only activity that felt worth doing during my holidays. Our relationship wasn't fickle, and I intended to keep it that way, but Father's plan put everything in distortion.

Before he left, he asked for a neighbour in university to tutor me – a preparation for junior secondary school. He said I needed to 'take this stage of life more seriously because it's the foundation of everything important'. Mother said to prepare for summer school and our departure to uncle's in the middle of August, precisely a week from now. Apart from feeling a bit antsy about leaving Yankee, I was unbothered by the move. While it meant I would have less time to spend with Yankee, it also meant I wouldn't have to see Father during the shorter breaks, like the Christmas break. It was also a relief that my relatives knew of my nightly inconveniences.

Done squeezing the sheets, I placed them in an empty bowl and dried them on the cloth line closest to the garden before pegging them. The last step before cleaning up was to pour the rinse and soapy water in the garden.

Hope the toxicity doesn't kill the trees.

As I tidied up and stacked the bowls back into a pile, the housekeeper opened the kitchen windows, took a peek as to what it was I was doing, then called to eat breakfast. Heeding, I hurriedly put the laundry bin in the stacked bowls and dashed for the room in fear of Mother seeing the wet and exposed side of the mattress. After placing the laundry bin in the passage connecting our room to our parents and the bowls back in the bathroom, I closed the door and dressed up for breakfast. Relieved I made it in time, I proceeded to the next course of action.

A bit more collected this time, I lifted the mattress to check if the other side was wet – it wasn't. Pleased, I used my last bit of strength to turn over the mattress, grunting in the process.

Mother was yet to come out of her room and so was Wande, but with breakfast ready time was insufficient. Proceeding with things, I took a stool, placed it by my wardrobe and reached for the top, took a pair of clean sheets, then dressed the bed.

Almost done, I heard Mother's door open, it was Wande. Her footsteps were distinctly different from Mother's, and with her leaving the room Mother was sure to follow, but there were still a few things left with too little time to do them.

Panicked, I hurried for the windows, opening them in a violent manner. I then reached for the fan control and increased the fan's speed from one to five before hopping on the bed, awaiting my cue.

One. two…After two seconds Mother came in.
On my knees we said our greetings and just as she turned to leave, she asked:

- She o ni wa jeun ni?
 Aren't you coming to eat?

    Mo n boo ma. *I'm coming ma.*

See no evil, know no evil.

Back on my feet, I straightened out the wrinkles on the sheet. Underneath it, I could see patterns of yesternight's incident and that of tonight and the night after. I was sure this new side of the mattress would, by the next day, become the old. Ever changing patterns that remind me of the worthlessness in living. I, unlike my sister, can't walk around in my nightwear as often, I can't wake up with the positive feeling of embarking on an adventurous day, I can't go to sleep without dreading the next morning. I can't dream of a future surrounded by either friends or strangers. I, unlike everyone in my family, have reasons to feel ashamed of my existence.

Back on the bed I felt enveloped in coldness, and I let it seep in. Slowly, it made its way into my bones, freezing and thawing them until they began to crack, until I could no longer take it and shielded myself with my blanket in hopes of forgetting all of it. In hopes of calmy sitting on the dinning without anyone paying my stench any notice. In hopes of the day I would no longer have to whisper prayers under my blanket, in hopes of these current whispers of mine reaching my creator and in hopes of my wishes reaching the grim reaper.

Who would believe if I told them my blanket knew more of my life than my parents. The secret wishes, sleepless and wet nights. It knows more than the adults that inhabit the room just two doors away. I sometimes ask myself *is it sadness or exhaustion I constantly feel?*

Any bystander would choose the former and I would the latter. It's like I once said to my dog;

I cannot feel sad for something or someone I cannot like.

During breakfast, all that could be heard was the youngest's incomprehensive chatter and Wande's complaint to turn on the TV. I sat opposite Mother on the other side of the table, assuming Father's position as the eldest since he returned to where he belonged. Mother asked which chocolate drink I wanted, I chose the usual – milo and milk.

While she mixed my drink, I helped myself with the bread and scrambled eggs. I presumed Mother already knew I did it again but chose to keep quiet about it.

…

> My mum puts me to sleep every night.
> My dad drives me to shopping rite on weekends..
> My grandma always lets me eat everything I want on holidays…

Three years ago, I conducted a self-inquiry, probably out of curiosity or due to boredom.

Other kids in school, boasted of how much love they felt from, thus towards, their parents but I couldn't relate. I, unlike them, felt neither comfort nor joy from being hugged by Father, rather I was beset by fear, discomfort, and unwillingness. When it comes to Mother, I have no memories of hugging or being hugged by her. Our set-in-stone interaction consisted mainly of me kneeling to say good morning then moving on to the next thing on my agenda. When we did talk, our conversation surrounded habits, studies, and Father.

The only thing I had in common with the kids, was the posed question by my parents on what it was I wanted for certain celebrations, like birthdays, Christmas and so on. But I already stopped requesting for things I really wanted at 6. After realising what it was I deeply desired and how incapable they were in giving it to me, I replied their questions with the ideal response.

I'm satisfied with whatever you give me.

I still remember how the discussion suddenly shifted to me.

> Ayo how about you?
> Her dad is cool, have you seen..
> I also heard he lives abroad and buys…

The discussion that day ended with the kids making assumptions as to how much I love my parents by basing them on the birthday celebrations, presents, gifts and fancy western outfits. When Mother picked us up that day, I stared at her hoping to arrive at some answers or at least feel something.

Nothing. All I felt was nothing. I was neither happy to see her nor was I happy she came to pick us up. I was only excited to return home to Yankee and was maybe a bit excited about getting to play feeding frenzy as it was Friday. After that day I constantly inquired for answers, but even after several months had passed, I had none. Tired of my pending response, I moved on to another question for which I had an immediate but dubious answer for.

For several months, my parents remained first in line, and despite having an answer I doubted it and refused to move on. The teachings of the children church gave me reasons to, so I repeatedly asked myself the same question to assure myself of its certainty. I got my first answer while petting my dog, just as I did the second, the third and those that followed.

Approximately two years have passed, and my answer remains unchanged. To say my parents love me would be a blatant lie since that is an emotion I haven't felt from, but more importantly towards them. The feeling is reciprocal; thus, the question in itself is unnecessary. If I cannot feel sad for someone I cannot like, it is also a given that my parents would feel no grief over my death.

Life is not a choice, not my choice and I have no desire to live it. I remember the first time I uttered those words aloud for myself, I felt relieved. I was relieved at the thought of a possibly closer and certain end. Relieved at the thought of my current sense of being, being retained. But death as since the onset been making a mockery of me. I can picture it saying to the grim reaper "this girl isn't worth our attention."

During the short years I have come to live, I have heard of many that "kicked the bucket" and prayed I was next in line, but this corrupt system has since the dawn of time always chosen the unwilling. Several lightbulbs pertaining how I could close the gap between me and the bucket did turn on from time to time, much more often than the lizards do our compound. But like the coward I am I have never dared to grab a hold of it, never dared to take charge of my fate. It was one excuse after another.

What if this height only leaves me crippled?
Is this not going to hurt.
God listens to obedient girls, I'll just wait our turn
Isn't this me betraying Yankee?
10 is the magic age.

At the vacation ceremony in school last month, I heard a parent's take on death while commenting on a celebrity's "improper conduct".

« Awon omode isin, bayen ni won maa ma le iku. Ti won ba di agba ni won maa ma sa fun iku. »
Kids of nowadays chase death without a second thought, unbeknownst to them is the twist of fate that awaits their adulthood.

It got me thinking, and I remember agreeing with her for a day or two, just like I do for most things they, the tall and grown, say. But then, I thought of how and why that could be applicable be to me in the future.

If death were to chase someone, why run from it?
Money?
Family?
Friends?
Fear?

I continuously kept myself busy with these options, weighing them. I concluded that none of them, as important as they might seem, could stop a desperate person. I also concluded that if death were ever to chase me, I will, just as I would now, welcome it with open arms.

But then again, options differ from person to person as do their importance. It is also unjust the way death deals with people. People without a diagnosed chronic illness, without any notice whatsoever, could suddenly drop dead. They would have no say in their death unlike suicidal people that decide the how and when. If left to me, I'd prefer the least painful death possible during the most boring moments of my life. It would not be as fulfilling to die during my moments of enjoyment, I might not protest but still it remains tragic, and is for me half the death. A death of that manner would mean I only had one foot in the boat before it took off, while the other foot remained on the shore, antsy to see that fun to the end. But does an unsatisfactory death mean half-death?

Their opinions aside, it is unfair. To one-sidedly change the rules of the game and make the chaser the chased. To opt out the game of chase and run just to, after regret, get pulled back in, and with the roles reversed. But that is life. The rules often favour forces beyond human reasoning, putting the human capability to reason and understand at a disadvantage. Two can't play the game called life. At this point, I must also acknowledge I feared the truth in the woman's words.

To die after finding peace shook the whole of me with fear but to stop now and continue living this life of mine, to continue living in fear, afraid of Father, afraid of my life's greatest inflictor of pain, all my life, was an even more dreadful thought.

As a kid, I calmed my troubled mind with only ifs, accompanying my fears.

Only if I wasn't born,
Only if they weren't my parents,
Only if I were not a coward and dared to give those lightbulbs the firmest grips of their lives.

…

I could see my reflection on the surface of the untouched tea, I could see myself frowning. I'm surrounded by happy people, yet I cannot share that happiness with them. I sometimes let myself go, I would relax and mingle with the crowd, get drawn in by the ambiance, but it has only left me with memories I'd rather throw in the bin and turn away from, with scars I have no understanding as to why I have them. With a life I cannot seem to understand.

Now being the only one left at the dining, I excused myself, carefully placed my dishes in the sink and left for the backyard. The tree provided shade, but I chose to lay on the bare floor two meters away from the garden, just far enough to reveal my healing and healed scars to the sun, but still close enough to receive its fallen leaves. Yankee laid by my side as I quietly watched the clouds slowly move and change forms.

A WALK IN THE RAIN

Since Father left two weeks ago and since the incident two months ago, we made a habit of spending time in the backyard, alone with Yankee, in peace.

It is after all quiet afternoons like this that make life worth living. It is here I discover myself.

*

> I'm greedy,
> I desire to shorten the trip to our certain end,
> to my certain end.
> Small and young as I am,
> I'm unable to accomplish a thing of desire.
> I can only think, dream, and hope.
>
>
> I'm crazy,
> I have voices in my head telling me how to live.
> I love them and want them to stay.
> They keep me sane.
>
> Ironic much.

---

* An extract from A.W.I.R poem

MEMORY: A GIFT AND A CURSE

- Debby, I have something for you.
  Wait, wait ... first you have to promise not to scream,
  your mom and your younger sister are yet to see it.
- *I promise.*

I briskly replied in anticipation of knowing what he had hidden in the car behind him.
Dad slowly opened the door and there she was. A brown puppy standing on all fours on the back seat, wagging its tail presumably from excitement.

Surprised, I looked at the puppy for a while before being overwhelmed by the eagerness to carry it.
I looked at father before reaching out.

- It's a she and she's a week old. Father added as the puppy sniffed and licked my fingers one by one.

I sat immobile beside her, giving her the time she needed to avoid scaring her away.

Within a minute, she slightly leaped into my arms before proceeding to lick my face. I first giggled, then gently carried her out of the car 'like she was an egg'. I was three, almost four, and the dog was a week old.

Out of the car, dad said to surprise mummy and Wande.

After closing the front door, we tiptoed our way towards mummy's room where she and Wande were. Daddy told me to wait in the living room by the passage to our bedrooms, opposite the bathroom.

First, he went to the bedroom on the left, to confirm Wande wasn't in our room, then to the right to lure out both mum and Wande.

The puppy was cooperative and kept quiet till Wande screamed upon seeing it.

Wande was the first to come out and was first to see the puppy. Upon seeing it, she immediately screamed and ran back to mummy. Mum came back with Wande in her arms, looking a bit worried because of the loud bark she heard and Wande's scream, but after seeing Yankee in my arms she laughed it off.

Mother still laughs when she, together with the rest of the family, reminisce about this fairytale.

I grew up hearing about it, seeing pictures of me constantly carrying Yankee in my arms, laughing with my parents, with Wande, with my cousins. I have images of how it could have played out in my head, and I accepted these images as the truth.

I am convinced that the day I wrote the name Yankee on the hardcopy of her first picture, I thanked father for adopting her. I'm convinced that the day we tiptoed the house, and scared

Wande, I thought father's plan was genius and had fun carrying it out.
I'm also convinced that these memories have been overridden by fear, hate, disappointment and lack of understanding.

It's like Father always says:
What people do not understand, they fear
and what they fear, they hate
and what they hate, they seek to destroy.

Never once could he have imagined that these thoughts and emotions would be directed at him.

It is farcical how I'm in another environment repeating the same thing as I did three months ago. Still the same wish with yet another wet face on yet another wet bed. I can see a mature version of me standing opposite me shaking her head in disapproval as she watches me shed these pointless tears of mine. God is probably up there yawning from boredom as I plead; saying *it's always the same old*.

As a kid I immersed myself in a lot of fantasy-based animated productions. Father downloaded as many as he could as souvenirs, Wande and I would sit by his laptop for hours binge watching each and every one of them, whenever we got the chance. Wande and I would laugh the scenes off, run to Father and narrate the storyline, showcasing our memory skills. We'd leave our parents room feeling proud of ourselves and sometimes sleep off while watching that episode that kept us glued to the screen. I'd wake up the next day, happy, only to, that same day, realise I had yet again made another mistake worthy of punishment.

Those days, those souvenirs were, in reality, moments of happiness I never truly could absorb. They went as soon as they came – happy one day, sore all over the next. Then, the fun outweighed the pain, and now it has all become trite – the once desired nostalgic feeling is gone, leaving behind realization and fear.

I realized I feared him. I feared not knowing when that happy moment could turn sour, I feared not knowing when those presents-giving hands could turn violent – or non-presents-giving legs for that matter. He repeatedly paints his actions as necessary since 'I'd previously and repeatedly been warned' but most of the times he punishes on impulse.
A fact to all but him.

His title "head of the house", his perfume – probably a German brand, his quirks of stomping around the house like a lion on hunt. All of it I have come to fear having around me. They meant discomfort, pain, hate, and sometimes murderous intent.

With time, I came to accept these fears as mine and we became one, they controlled my actions and I let them. I neither smiled nor talked more than necessary when he visited. Once I heard him say to mom:

O ti n ko eyin awon omo si mi abi?
You're turning the kids against me, aren't you?

I wondered if it ever crossed his mind that he could be at fault, that he, maybe just maybe, was as guilty as mom for 'turning me against him'. That maybe what he actually needed was to come to his senses and look at the kid in front of him, than at those out on the street or on the news. But none of that matters now. What matters is what I realised – what made me find peace within myself. It sunk in that my situation wasn't one to cry about.

I realised that no matter how much pity I feel for myself, it changes nothing, no matter how much I cry, it changes nothing, no matter how much I pray, it has changed nothing and will therefore change nothing.

My solitude brought me peace, it prevented me from getting swooped in by the ambiance generated from his arrivals, it held me back from being carried away by his presents and instead steered me in the right direction, prepared me for the arrival of his true nature. It unblinded me and showed me what I had.

My reality is to continue the trip on this train with no influence on its direction, my fate is to for aeons have no hands in my fate. Father will, after all forever decide all and convince himself he's doing it all for my sake.

It has been two months since I was sent to experience this jail of a place in his stead. We have only had an on-the-phone-contact once. I requested for the call, and during the call I pleaded to be pardoned – to be let out of this jail.

There were times I sought for the o n e guilty of my situation, but it's unbeknownst to me who the source of my birth is. I once believed there was dove that came into a darkness but *who created that darkness* was the question that followed. I reached a dead end.

I have cried, I have in fact also prayed my pains out and it has done nothing but scar me even more. On the wood supporting the mattress right above me, I can visualise my prayers, pleas, and pains upon a dunghill, I can see how they desperately came out my mouth only to be deposited by the wind of hopeless cases.

'*Non-existent in my life*' is the perfect phrase to describe whoever it was I relied on for help and the I in the whole. If there's someone that helps those deemed worthy of help, then that someone remains non-existent to me. Present in others' lives but absent in mine. Then there is me.

Not once have I had control of the events in my life, hence hindered from taking the obvious route. The moment I mention the word poison is the moment I'd be taken to the chapel for deliverance, asked to fast and plead for forgiveness, looked at with pitiful and maybe spiteful eyes, then doomed to forever be reminded of it by my family members in a negative light. Although I could despite this, proceed with taking matters into my own hands, but who would give a child poison even if she politely asked? The only help I could get was within me and therein I sought for help, yet therein I found none.

A relative once told me, "Expectations lead to disappointment – for one to get disappointed then they must have expected something to begin with".

If I were to momentarily believe in that, that would mean I never expected something from the one, or ones, who brought me to this market called life, from those who left me to cater to my own needs, those who left me in the hands of a couple or literatim in the palm of their hands.

As of now I cannot bring myself to hate them, but I do hope that I will one day. I see it as my driving force, but also as a threshold withholding me from actively reaching out to death. A little yet meaningful purpose to help me go by yet another miserable morning of living – a thing I loathed when others, like Wande, carelessly and carefreely did, thus a thing I never wanted to do. But as always, Father drives me to the edge and makes me do things I never would have imagined.

The morning bell rang, causing the mirage that stared me in the face to disappear, bringing me back to reality. I woke up from my death pose with no zeal to think.

Just like I have been programmed to, I took a bowl of water brushed my teeth with some paste and my index finger, took a quick shower, put on my house wear, took my prayer book and headed for the chapel for the 30-minute morning prayer.

5:55am, 25 minutes since the bell rang – an intro into the day's continuous agenda. First is the gathering at the chapel for the morning prayer at 6:00, consisted by some prayers songs from the prayer book, and some extra information from the hostel masters or mistresses.

05:56. Four more minutes left. More than a few were missing. During the next three minutes that followed, out-of-breath students made their way into the chapel. Particularly disturbing were those that made it seconds before the clock struck six and moments before the giant doors got shut.

06:00. With the doors shut, it was time. The chapel prefect went to the altar and asked all to rise, while trying his best to be louder than the whips outside.

06:05. Some juniors with tears in their eyes made their way in. Behind them were seniors that once sourced the envy of juniors like me – the females had their hands proudly displayed by their sides and the males had theirs in their pockets. Both walked in with a false sense of dignity. A month was all I needed to know that.

The choir continued unbothered by the new entrée of students and sang with pride. It was flawless and melodious despite the odd time and ridiculous display of authority that just took place behind closed doors. Adaptation is a scary thing.

> Thank God for the things he's done for us.

A sentence that puts the hymn singing to a conclusion and commences the prayer session. The chapel prefect says a line and we repeat after him.

> Thank God for his mercy.
> We thank you Lord for keeping us alive and healthy.
> We thank you Lord for keeping us safe from all harm.
> We thank you Lord for the life you have blessed us with.
>
> Cover us with the blood of Jesus.... the blood of Jesus.
> We are grateful for all you have done for us.

I unlike or like these people share none of these thanks. To me, mercy means saving me from my horror, from my shame, granting me death thereby giving me something to be grateful for.

A simple wish was all I asked for. People die daily and amongst them are those that are unwilling, all I wanted was an exchange – mine for one.

Back home the prayers always begin the same way. Our youngest would start with 'Thank you lord for keeping us alive' and the younger with, 'Thank you lord for forgiving us of our sins' and I made sure to either thank him for those I knew had it well or those that seemed to have it well. Series of thanks that had nothing to do with me. Regardless, I did my best to ensure mine was the longest of us three – which was what mattered.

This sucks,
is what I would have said if I wanted a smack on the back my head, but otherwise that summarises what I think about all mornings since I came here. We wake up 5:30a.m only to, after a long day of school and a one-dimensional schedule, sleep at 22:00p.m.

*Spend a fortune get a pe*a
is what I prefer to call my life here, but Father says the money is worth it. He calls it something I remember as a preparation centre, in Father's words 'a place of luxury'. Either way I think

of here as a place that would fulfil the function he, as a parent, is unable to.

He demands for me to appreciate his efforts, as this is 'a place of luxury he never had the **opportunity** to experience', with emphasis on the opportunity. I, on the other hand, find it difficult to connect this place to the word luxury and I certainly do not see my being here as an opportunity. But then again, people like Father just refuse to see reality. His dream was all that ever mattered.

Just why am **I** here?

Because Father made me

Did you plead otherwise?
Of course I did
Then what did he say?
He asked why by remaining silent
Then what did you say?

I said I was bored.

You see, that's where you were wrong!

This place breeds pariahs, masochists, sadists and even more sadists. Which means after 6 years, we'll have a total of 30 pariahs and/or masochists and 33 sadists – females and maybe some males – that have been produced in the name of raising children, just to be released into society by their parents in the hopes of doing them and the country some good. But of course, if telling Father this was going to change anything, that would be a slap on my face through the phone.

Only 20 minutes had passed, but it feels like I had been switching between standing and sitting for an eternity.

How annoying. When will this end?
I wish the day was already done with. Or even better a time stop.

A time stop would be a big change of plans – not like it is humanly possible. Moreover, it would require a high degree of selfishness to wish for it with all my heart. Ironically enough, being selfish is a quality I lack, which I find rather astonishing. It makes me wonder if it is possible for a desperate person to lack selfishness. They are either not desperate enough, or they just haven't found the need and/or absolute necessity to be selfish.

It saddens me to realise I do not consider my current situation that of absolute necessity – following the same daily routine, like a robot with switches only to be controlled not by oneself but by the teachers, the reverend sisters, headmistresses and masters.

Am I happy being controlled?

To leave this hostel has, for the past two months, been a dream of mine. Literally. Once I dreamt of it getting burnt to the ground, becoming nothing but heaps of ashes, ending with everyone having to go home. Although it's no happy ever after, I prefer it.

Father's punishments were only during his visits, but hostel meant every second of my life in school.
No hostel, no teachers.
No hostel, no headmasters.
No hostel, no collective punishment, no hell canes, no foreign drivers of my train.

In an attempt to be optimistic, I constantly try to convince myself of my desperation by considering how my desires managed to seep their way into my unconsciousness, but it has always been hard to not be pessimistic. It is hard to ignore the possibility of not thinking of my current situation as that of absolute necessity.

I have always thought I could safely rely on myself, but with how things have turned out, that thought just seems to have met its demise – therein any future thoughts of a plan B or C. I have always told myself that relying on someone else would most likely lead to failure. But now it seems relying on myself could have the same outcome.

It's pathetic, really.

Surviving hostel without getting a beating is impossible, but surviving with one's sanity intact is possible. A senior in her sixth year, *SSS3, once told her me her trick to 'lasting this long'.

'It will be over before I know it'.

That was what she repeatedly told herself since her first year, *JSS1. Silently, she'd chant it as her mantra when the seniors ordered her to do their chores.
When she together with the whole hostel got punished mainly because the culprit refused to come forward and acknowledge their crime, and partly because "snitches get stitches".
When she got flogged for coming a few seconds late to the evening prayers. Afterall a beating before prayer keeps the kid in the kid at bay.

To me her trick was more of a lie than a trick. With every rising morning, I live an eternity of a day just to relive another. It may have helped her cope with her situation, but it certainly wouldn't me. If anything, it would plunge the whole of me into chaos since I don't function that way.

After the passing of each birthday, I surprise myself by celebrating yet another birthday healthier than, or just as healthy as, the previous. But I don't go thinking 's*o this much time has passed'*. My life in between those birthdays always

---

*SSS3 -Senior Secondary School 3
*JSS1 – Junior Secondary School 1

felt like an eternity and I remember them as such. It leaves me feeling hopeless; dreading living yet another eternity.

Oblivious, my family puts a lot of effort into making my birthdays land on the top of my list of best days. For them, that day marks the day they got the first child they so much longed for. According to Father I was the joy that came into their lives, the item that unbranded mom from being called barren after three years of marriage with no child.

Mom made efforts to invite as many family members and family friends as she could which I appreciated since some, or rather, one of them were fun to have around. Father made efforts to pay for the expenses and physically celebrate with us, an effort he would like more appreciation for, but one I never once appreciated as he never once missed it, with today being an exception.

I have against my will lived this long and with how things are playing out even today, on my hopefully *last **last** last birthday* as I called it last year, I will most likely continue to live the next five years of my life in this hellhole – just like she did but without a trick.

With a grunt from my seating partner on the left, I relieved my partner on the right from its duty of supporting my weight. All in standing ovation, I awaited our turn to join the march to the dormitory. The males, closest to the main doors, commenced the march and were first to leave. After a while, the females joined the march. Receiving my cue, I took on my don't-bother-me look and marched on.

A WALK IN THE RAIN

It's the same every morning. Hell bell 1 strikes at 05:30a.m and we are forced to wake up. It strikes again at 06:59a.m and the most of us run amok. Most seniors try to get some of that perfume on before it's too late, and most juniors run straight for the refectory. They know what's good for them after all.

Two series of strikes and our morning as hostellites is put to an end. The third is heard from another source. Hell bell 2. A bell for all.

Walking towards the dormitory, I could see the bread deliverer park his car by the kitchen. I moved my face up and I could see the sky making way for the sun. I looked at my wristwatch. 06:33. We have an atom-of-time to bathe per usual.

As we marched, I gave the sky a closer look. Looking closer I could see a few stars and the never smiling moon. The stars looked so peaceful, slowly fading away. The view never gets old. It reminds me of old times that barely date three months back. Old times that are forever existent in my body, mind, and soul.

I further my walk, or rather, our march back to the dorm in a mechanical way. It's easy really, after some months in school, my legs seem to know when to turn and when to stop, with the help of my peripheral vision alone.

It is no more pleasant than it would have sounded if someone had said that to me before I came here. No stress, no thoughts.

All that is involved is abiding by the set rules and living by the different time slots. It's no different from my life outside this place. Moreover, I came here to fulfil my obligations towards my parents and my society. To be here means to have obligations, to be trained to fulfil those obligations, to think about and see nothing but those obligations. But to call those obligations mine is however another matter. I was brought here to live by Father's take on my obligations and meet the expectations he has of me, to understand the reason without being told, to thank him later without really understanding why.

After returning my prayer book, I hurried to the backyard to take yesterday's dried up underwear from the cloth line. With the pegs in one hand and the singlet and pant in another, I headed for my wardrobe, took my bowl, placed the sponge, soap, toothpaste and toothbrush in it and headed for the veranda just beside the backyard. Luckily my bucket remained untouched.

I took it as their way of celebrating my birthday. It felt nice to be spared of an extra concern as to what to bathe with, like the owners of the almost emptied up buckets around mine. I remembered seeing those buckets just the night before, I remember them being filled up when I took a scoop from mine just this morning. We all have our crosses to bear, as little as they may sometimes seem.

Underwear,

water,

soap,

pegs. Here everything is up for grabs if left in the open for too long. 'Too long' could be minutes, it could be seconds. It differs from thief to thief.

Friday means sportswear, school, extracurricular activities, and 'fun' hostel activities. I despise these things. While we hopelessly study 21:00-22:00p.m, I'd rather while away my time looking at the stars. Instead of being seen as the weird one out for not smiling or laughing as easily during extracurricular activities, I'd rather be cuddled up on my bed. I'd rather spend my weekend running around the compound with Yankee, than get flogged or acknowledged by my teachers for my school performance. I would rather cease to exist than breathe. But life's not a choice, it never was and never will be.

06:45. After putting on my singlet, pant and sportswear, I brushed my newly shaved hair, put on my beret and was about to close my all-purpose cupboard before realising I was yet to take a pair of socks. Scanning all over in search of my socks, I realised my cupboard looked appealing. The provisions were by the right and wears were by the left in an open space, the ironed ones on the hangers and the bed sheets and my extra set of house wear and school uniform were right below them. Just beside that, on the other side of the plank of wood, built into the cupboard for orderly division, were the provisions; stacked up in an orderly manner – separated and shared into four mini compartments. I had barely touched mine and that in itself was appealing as the ***begging season*** was approaching. An event of lavish eaters for lavish eaters.

With just a month and two weeks gone, they would have gobbled up most, if not all, their provisions and will seek to fill their 'tummies and cupboards with others'. One of the very few useful knowledge I obtained from the tour on my first day here.

The begging season.
As the term suggests the plea begins with some flattery, puppy eyes and some joking around, the main distinction between this term and the dictionary definition of begging is the change in demeanour once one refuses to give in – if the beggar encounters a strong-willed junior, they resort to violence and coerce the junior into giving in. Threats, blackmail, lies, anything is possible for them, as long as their goal is reached. In simple terms, the seniors "politely ask" the younger ones for some extra milk, cereals, sugar, or cassava flakes after having used up theirs. She who refuses will be worked to her bones. It is the real life in this mini. Adultcracy.

I left my cupboard with a pair of white socks in hand and headed for the table in front of our hostel.

06:53. I sat on the wooden table by the veranda, put on my socks, and took my polished shoes I, earlier on, left to dry.

06:55. I went to my bunk, took my hymnbook, school bag, and headed for my classroom, feeling exhausted.

Just like Father said, my being here was never to have fun but to learn and make the best of this luxury. One he never had the opportunity to enjoy as a kid.
Hate it as I may, I will come to thank him later, he said.
Kids never know what's good for them, he said.

I tried different methods to make this hell bearable. I fought, I convinced myself I was wrong, and that Father is always right, I have somehow managed to not bawl to Mother and beg her for my freedom during our two phone calls so far, I didn't make a fuss like other kids my age nor have I had an outburst.

I have repeatedly told myself *go to sleep*, but eternal sleep never came. I thought it obvious that life just thought hell on earth was the fitting punishment for a nuisance like myself. The harder I tried; the harder life was. The more effort I put into living; the more hardships life gave. It was one after the other.

Life never cared about my thoughts, I was nothing but an insignificant pebble that could be used and sacrificed for its greater good – whatever that was. It took me a while, but I learnt my lesson and I learnt it the harder way. The lesson was simple – it hurts less when you see the bad times coming and to me Father was life. Life would rather watch me experience the worst of the worst until I have neither the zeal nor the will to rise back to my feet.

Although Father is life, life isn't Father. Father is a form of life, but he carries out life's will. Father is life's way of putting me in my place, making me experience all sort of experiences; bitter, sweet, good, bad, sour, bittersweet.

Through Father, life gave me someone to love – someone that loved me in return – just to put me in a world where our love was not accepted. We loved in secret and that was enough, at least for a while. Now the only source of anything and everything positive in my life is, once again, Yankee.

06:57. I left my class with gentle but quick steps and headed towards the refectory. Decorum is expected.

To the rest of the school, we hostellites are the epitome of conventionality – at least that is what we are supposed to be. Although mostly left unsaid, it is what we were sent here to become.

In school, we are a sales pitch, an item of curiosity and admiration for the day students. We are to wherever we are beam of perfection, with properly ironed school wear, snow-white socks, an ever clean or new school bag, an untorn and smooth hymn book, neat low cut with an oversized yet idealised beret to top it. These things were to define us that represented and presented the school's pride – hostellites. We were proof of a top-class care and training.

We were proper and proper was the rage among parents.

06:59. The whole school echoed with the second series of strikes, and I was in the final destination of all that is to come.

Hell bell 1's message was loud and clear, but it was easy to miss the bell's most important detail. I have come to understand, from earlier observations, that the time prefect and wielder of the bell moves his hand a bit too similarly to the headmaster's. The strength they put into wielding their different weapons synchronise. I thought it a result of the male's hostel mood, since it never happened when the tenure of power switched over to the female's hostel. According to this theory, today's strikes will be particularly strong.

I'm sure that when the authorities chose to enforce a hard penalty for late coming, they thought, 'this will surely increase punctuality and would most definitely show the school's strictness and top-tier class care'. But ironically enough, the hell bells strike fear and confusion into their recipients. The bell throws all care for decorum out the window, leaving nothing but chaos and desperation behind. It lays bare the ugly reality of being an hostellite.

7:00a.m. Already inside the refectory, I prepare myself for breakfast and set up the table for my pack, while avoiding the ugly sight of desperate kids running like there's no tomorrow with the typical appearance, belts halfway in, berets looking like the Eiffel tower, shoelaces browner than ever and the day kids watching them with their mouths slightly agape. The everyday spectacle hell bell 1 brings with its final sound.

Last to enter unscathed is the welder of hell bell 1, the hostel's timekeeper. He delivers hell cane hostel to its impatient wielder and proceeds into the refectory for a sumptuous breakfast.

How can he manage to stomach anything?

To answer that I need to ask myself how **I** can stomach my food, and how I can bear to lick the hot stew off my fingers before proceeding to dip the bread in again while hearing the lashes of hell cane h. on the backs of both the feeble and strong. So much for an unwanted luxury, and as said future sadists, or maybe just bystanders – passive and active alike.

Both hell bells and all hell canes got their names when I fell at hell cane hostel and hell bell 1's mercy. Just a few hops and jumps away and I would have been safe. I would be sitting with my pack, watching on as hell cane did its job, I would have continued to see the cane as a product of a tree and the bell a product of iron and I too as made of iron.
But that day I fell, literally.

Afraid, I hid behind the other latecomers. One by one, they received their punishment, and I dreaded mine. As I watched the others, I realised that the knee length pinafore and the short sleeve shirt left too many areas bare. I dreaded my fate. The dread of my impending kismet increased with every lesser hostellite I could hide behind. But as life had it, with some yells from my comrades, my unavoidable fate came, and it was my turn. The first hit was on my left forearm.

Hell cane h. bore its way into the skin of my left forearm, and I remember the pain lasted throughout breakfast. While I ate, I couldn't think about anything but the throbs on my butt, forearm and back. It was fast but painful. It formed a melody; the melody of my nightmares.
Tap, taptap, taptaptaptaptap, ... tap.

If I were to compare, Father's wire hurts two hells more. Assuming hell got worse the deeper you dive into it, Father must be the governor of the very end, at the lowest layer next to lava. His beatings had neither melody nor staccato, they were as distorted as his behaviour. I never understood the patterns.

For the seniors, these punishments are merely a talent show. They neither cry nor wimp, the elasticity of the hell cane doesn't budge them, not in the slightest. It's their way of showing that they can, under no circumstances, be bossed around and that they couldn't be less bothered by a thing such as a hell cane – agreeable but not yet achievable.

For the teachers, this is a display of authority, one they maybe lack outside school and arguably in school. The most flexible hell cane is their favourite, it bounces off as soon as it lands, leaving a red mark on the darkest and thickest of skin. It bounces off then returns with double the force – real hell for the juniors. They are slow, not so calculative, they have little endurance and burst into tears almost immediately.

Thank God that isn't me, is surely what most of the juniors sitting in here are thinking as they steal a few glances at those at the cane's mercy. A circus show at its best.

This jungle is not only about survival of the fittest, but also survival of the smartest. Smart juniors can easily get by harsh mornings like this even if they lacked the spine. Getting into the refectory before hell bell 1 stops is just one of the many challenges of a hostellite's daily routine, and there are special cases when we could receive more than we are due.

After the hostel master gives out hell cane's blessings, the last latecomer is to head to their table and receive glares for having delayed the group's breakfast.

Each table is a pack of its own, if a member is missing, the rest must wait their arrival before commencing breakfast. The more in need of hell cane's blessing, the more one needs to avoid making eye contact with. Not to mention, after the wait eating becomes a crime to the rest of the pack.

Unlike them, I was free from that agony. Done eating, I placed my plate in an empty sink, beside the other two sinks filled with heaps of plates – the business of the refectory team for the week.

Through the net-like long rectangular window screen above the eight sinks, I spotted the headmaster headed to the hostel to return hell cane h., he seemed relaxed.

For shame, I thought.

For hostellites, being flogged is one punishment and being flogged outside is another. We are like animals on display, the regulars know we exist, they adore our beautiful appearances, the aroma our refectory emits every morning and afternoon. But because it is believed that only the rotten apples are beaten, the punished loses all respect and adoration – if they ever had any to begin with. Most impacted are those that try to save face, they end up wishing they never tried.

I returned to my classroom, the first class in the building opposite our refectory. Its location has proven to be as convenient as it isn't. In front of it is the refectory, behind it the chapel. To its left are the other JSS1 classes; y and z, to its right is the poorly built hostel kitchen and in front of that is the male dormitory, that is partly connected to the next building – the female's hostel. Thus deemed the most ideal place to study during the evenings, before lights out and after dinner, which is after the evening prayers. One slight mistake in one of these stages, and it sticks.

Some of my classmates were already seated in their respective seats by the time I got in. I waved my greetings to a few and headed to my seat.

07:17. 13 minutes before hell bell school or two strikes. Just like for hostel, the dos and don'ts are obvious but are for some hard to comply with. A hymn book, proper looks – short hair and fairly ironed uniform – and short nails will do the trick. Anything short of that and it's hell cane two with a bonus of tiny stones on the knees.

By the window, on my seat, I could see the green grass separating my class from the chapel and the school's rear gate – one of the hostellite's forbidden fruits – in a parallel manner. On the other side of the chapel is the dunghill.

The school is built to mimic the stages in life. Starting from the rear gates, the buildings connect making a systematic interconnectedness with each other as they increase in level the further one walks up to the front gate. Just beside the main gate is the SS1 and 3 building, years when most choose to either boost themselves out of secondary school by taking the GCE-exams or graduate the proper way by receiving their secondary school diplomas.

07:29. The school's time prefect makes her way down to our class to cover the whole school.

Heeding the bell's call, I left the rest of my belongings behind in the classroom and headed for the assembly with my hymn book in hand.

The assembly consists of 36 lines of students starting from the females in the junior classes JSS1x, y and z and ending with the males in the senior classes SSS3 Science, Arts and Commercial. Behind every class is a prefect – the school's effort to be time efficient with rooting out its weeds of the day.

07:30. The prefects begin to position themselves behind each class, preventing any late comer from joining the line and officially signalling the start of the morning assembly. 07:31. The morning praise and worship begins. Anyone running to their class's line at that time is considered a latecomer and is to kneel on pebbles until the assembly's concluded by a few words from the vice principal.

Drums, piano, flute, national anthem, cockroach-like voices, and extra information from the vice principal are the mains of the assembly – for most. There are other things to focus on when one has to convince the prefect to let things slide for the day, after confirming it's another prefect, just to use the same excuses as the day before. If it is the same prefect, the next course of action is to sneak into the other class's line. If they succeed, then it's a mental feat and maybe something to brag about. But if they fail, it's a loss with some scars to prove it.

Occupied with my thoughts, I didn't notice the prefect standing beside me. He had to tap on my shoulder to inform me of his presence. The only detectable thing about him was the stern look he had on his face which was seemingly directed at me.

I was first in line, thus last to be inspected.

MEMORY: PAINS AND REGRETS

That night.

I loved the silence of the night, the wind, the Christmas lights that was on all year round, Yankee's fur and the never smiling moon. Without these in my life, love remained non-existential.

Everything was planned so well that I didn't notice a thing. I didn't notice I was being deceived. Deceived into living a life of Father's for Father. I thought it was worth it, studying far away from Yankee since it meant far away from him.

Afterall, his visits were mostly limited to where his family was and for six years, I would be a part of a relative's family 2-hour drive away from home, in another state.
At least that was what I thought when he informed me of the move to my new school. I considered his pride that would prevent him from visiting as often as he normally would home. It was well thought out on my part, but unfortunately my plan only came to fruit in my head.

That night, we were alone outside. In the front yard, on the boot of Mother's red Mercedes Benz.

Hesitant to leave I kept on hugging her, I could feel her wet fur against my face, and I could hear her panting louder than usual. I refused to let go, the only decision I'm allowed to make is whether I should leave without saying our proper goodbyes or not.

I promise not to forget you and I promise to ask to visit as often as I can. It's also impossible to have fun anywhere else if you're not in it...
I really will miss you.

She may or may not have understood everything I said to her, but I felt better after she licked me before taking off on her adventure. That alone was enough to bring me to tears.

Worry comes with love. It's like the bread with its crumbs, a deal with the devil and its price, like a special package accompanying the main one, of which the former carries more wight than the latter.

My parents were not worried, at least not Father. Throwing a 9-year-old into a den of lions when he had the cheaper option, the safer route. Rather he chose to put me in the hands of prestige, religion and what not. All in his attempt to solidify his role as the head of the house in the eyes of those who know him. A redundant course of action.

Without me at home,
who would carry her when she runs out the gate? Who would take her on a race around the compound? Who would dispose of the lizards she refuses to bury just because their guts were splattered? It seemed reckless leaving her in their hands, they

don't know the first thing when it comes to taking care of a dog, of her. All they do is ruffle her fur every now and then, and chain her when a visitor comes visiting.

Six years with her and they have learnt nothing.

What would happen to her without me, would my younger sister be able to take proper care of her, she has a strength the size of an ant. We are a year and a half apart and I'm way stronger than her. I was in a slight state of panic, but all I could do was worry till it was time to head in.

After a while bedtime came and Mother yelled to head in. Although it was earlier than usual, I understood we were to leave at dawn to avoid traffic – they were especially worse on Sundays.

After giving her a tummy rub, I headed in, prepared for bed and went to sleep. The next day, I left without saying goodbye.

Maybe if I had given her a hug, I wouldn't be feeling as enveloped in pain and regret as I am now.
But I was oblivious.

I thought it was a given – where I would be living. Mother never said anything good about our primary school's boarding students. She said it was a breeding ground for waywardness. I guess they thought Catholicism made a difference.

Mother did you know we could, after graduating, become future social pariahs? Was that your intention?

Did you intend for us to be unable to relate to anything but inside jokes, ones that only people with experiences just like ours understand. Did you ever imagine that the gap between you and I would only widen if we spent years apart. Did you ever think of the consequences your actions could have had, or were you just yet another insignificant figure – voice – in your own marriage, in comparison to your husband's.

I don't blame myself for whatever decision I made during my stay there. I know better than to do that. Rather I blame them. I blame them for birthing me and using me as they pleased. But then again, kids to them are like disposal cans – like an investment but disposable if not utilisable – and dogs like decorating materials.

November 2013

Time pass me not by, please wait and let me pass you by said a foolish 10-year-old on her birthday a few days ago. The same day she realised her pleas have long since been thrown into the bin. Hanging onto her last crumb of faith, she whimpered *lord save me* for the last time. This she did on her two and a half bed in a fairly large room with 63 others all bound to suffer the same life for a period of one to six years; the sentence was six, and some had served a portion of theirs.

2 words came to mind as I watched her:
ridiculous and pathetic.

There she laid, still as ever in her own urine, an apparent result of her carelessness, but she looked so unbothered, and it left me wondering if her olfactory lobe was functioning. I kept on watching as she remained immobile, as she looked lifeless while tears nonchalantly flowed from both outer corners of her eyes to the only dry item on her bed, the pillow.
After a short while of silence, she moved. An uncharged effort to drag her body back up until it was against the wall.

All but her were asleep, but she looked like she didn't care if anyone saw her. So I watched on.
I watched how her eyes let out tears in correspondence with her nose, how they met to form one heavier stream down her previously plump cheeks. The mixture of both on her face was pure horror, but I couldn't take my eyes off her. So I watched on.

It was obvious she had been awake for a while and that she was fed up. Her tears most likely stemmed from sadness, desperation, ignorance, anger seemingly directed towards something – but that is nothing but a speculation.

I could only guess as she left me on the sidelines just like she did you. She left us watching and refused to let us in. Her face bore no emotion and lost eyes looked even more lost. I wanted to remind her we existed for her, but I knew she knew, and that there was no point telling her a fact that is embedded in her soul. So I watched how she slowly faded away.

Minutes passed and our connection with her remained broken. Slowly, she began to think, she wanted to merge with me and succeeded. Prior to this I could hear myself say with her:
WHAT MORE IS THERE TO DO, CONTINUE LIVING?

She thought, why... why? She asked herself the same question over and over, but I gave no response. I had none, no reason came to mind. Although we were one again, I have yet again failed to produce results. I proclaimed myself guilty.
I made her crumble, fall apart, shatter.

She stands, takes off the soiled sheet, stuffs it in her shoe rack takes another of the same colour, wipes the wet mackintosh sheet with her pillowcase before protecting her mattress. Done with the deed, she returned to the same position with her back against the wall.

Mother and Father once mentioned in a discussion;
"kids are kids because they do not hold grudges".

Apparently this one isn't a kid. I could feel the anger in her
tears, her movement gave it all out. You couldn't help but feel
sorry for her, you stretched your hand to help as she headed for
the bathrooms, but then we locked eyes. A simple look was
enough, I gestured, and you understood. All of this, the
suffering, the neglect, the hate, we need to let all of it sink into
that thick skull of hers.
It's for her own good, she needs this.

Hate, anger, revenge, disgust, death.
Death, disgust, revenge, anger, hate.

Oblivious to her, these are her oxygen, and they must remain
that way. Take it away and you have an empty barrel. Those
tend to make the loudest of sounds, they tend to hurt most on
the inside. Our purpose is to help her.

Back home, we once heard in the church:
Earth is a market, and heaven is home.

Although sent to the market against her will, she has bought
what we thought necessary ages ago, but home never came to
her. Home ignored her pleas; home pushed her to the edge.
Countless times we have said go, just take matters into your
hands and go home. But we hate pain and so does she. She
constantly mumbles how movies make it look so easy when it
actually isn't.

Thinking is one thing and doing is another, she'd say.

A WALK IN THE RAIN

We have thought out several options for her – the painful but quick ones, and she executed none. What to do with this hopeless child.

*

> I'm endowed with scars from earlier efforts to be set free.
> The direction we are headed is the only gleam of hope I have left.
>
> Death.

TILL NEXT TIME OR NOT

---

* Extract from the poem A.W.I.R

I looked up without smiling and expected him to repeat what he said since I obviously didn't hear him. He seemed to be losing his patience but that didn't bother me, all he needed to do was just to repeat what he said. But then again, it is the pride that comes with the position at work. No one to inspect the inspector. No one to punish Father the way he does me.

Sometimes what goes around doesn't always come around Father.

I tucked my hymnbook under my armpit and showed my nails. He seemed like he wanted to say something but turned around. After his departure his existence became a thing of the past and a few minutes after so did the morning assembly. The school band started playing and I commenced the juniors' march to the class being the first in line and belonging to JSS1x.

Classes have always performed the same function for me.
In class, I learned, played and most importantly cried.
In class students sometimes make friends, and even more often than necessary betrayed friends.

Currently my class is starting to liken hell. I'm situated on a desk, butt faced up and head faced down, the typical position for scapegoats. While I do agree that there are times when a scapegoat is deserving of their punishment, I also acknowledge there are times when they aren't.

Prior to today, I've felt bad for these scapegoats, but right now as I'm on display for a crime in which I could be proven innocent for, only if the teacher gave my words any credit, I feel more than pity for myself. I am for the second time in one morning exposed to the pride that comes with a position of power and authority. I'm keeping count, its necessary.

Even if it is a common occurrence, it is unnecessary and barbaric. I was accused by a fellow house mate, thereby a trustworthy source. It can be likened to being called out by a family member for a wrongdoing, their words were taken with utmost trust.

According to the information that has undergone several transitions – first from the hostel mate, the headmistress, then the parents of the victim in my accusation, then the principal, then this teacher – I have accused her, the teacher, of beating up a sick asthma student for something *as trivial as neglecting her homework* even though she knew the student was sick. She said this while mimicking my tone and stressing the part of the homework and its triviality.

The student, now known as victim, is an hostellite. Her sickness worsened after she was beaten by the teacher, to the extent that her parents were asked to come pick her up. All I did was state the fact that she was beaten by a teacher before her condition worsened, but what the parents got to hear was that a teacher was responsible for intentionally maltreating their child.

What happened after is easy to guess, the headmistresses got called out by the parents for their negligence, who must also have, after that, proceeded to inform the school authorities about it. The headmistresses got called by the principal or vice principal for further explanation and they, with the intention of excluding themselves from the whole, narrowed the whole issue to me, the informant, and the teacher, the culprit.

I'm certain all this teacher got to hear was how horrible of a teacher she is to have put a kid on a sick bed by being irrational, and that if not for the kindness of **student who** – an uncalled-for title – they would never have known of her true character and ended the 'discussion' with a warning.

Obviously, she didn't take it well. She probably got angry thinking she only did what she thought was right, and most likely convinced herself that she knew nothing of the girl's sickness despite her cries and pleas that day. The anger could also have stemmed from being close to losing her job. But overall, anger is all I can see in those eager eyes as she scanned my body in search of defenceless areas while telling of the 'terrible injustice she has come to suffer thanks to me'. At that moment she had an uncanny resemblance to Father.

They both claim they are doing right by showing their take on what is right and what is wrong, an essential difference that must be mastered to ensure a bright future they'd say, when in fact what they do is abuse their given authority to calm the fury in them by using whatever or whoever they think is convenient.

In her hand was the best hell cane the school had to offer, she borrowed it from the teacher next door. He said her purpose was of utmost importance, compared to his – he was to punish those that failed to submit their homework to the class captain. I can see him smirking as he watches from window before coming to his senses and reminding himself to chase his students back to the classroom. He threatened to flog anyone he sees outside once he had the ultimate instrument back in his hands before resuming his position by the window.

'Now all of you should learn from this one', she said as she landed the first hit.

I was on the verge of tears before the first one came; all it did was push something that already existed. She moved from the back to the butt, as the sound wasn't enough proof for her that the strikes hurt. Although it hurt more on the butt, she regardless moved to the legs, but that didn't suffice either, so she danced around as she accused me of disrupting the lesson, of wasting the time of everyone present in the room and that of the teacher next door. I pleaded innocent.

Her anger left scars on my knees and my behind; the back of my legs, my buttocks and my back. She refused to stop despite my pleas. If the pleas did anything, they only worsened my situation. When she showed no signs of stopping, I stopped with the pleas, all I could do was cry until she flogged all her anger out.

Satisfied with my screams and with the audience by the windows, she asked to plead for forgiveness from my classmates. The how and reason was for me to guess.

It was simple. On my knees I was to plead for wasting their time. As I grovelled on my knees, my classmates turned away. I was sure I looked pathetic, dragging my knees from chair to chair with mucus dangling down my nose and fresh tears turning dry.

Done grovelling round the class, she seemed satisfied and returned the cane to its owner who immediately used it to chase the stubborn spectators back to their classes. I was ordered to stand for a while and during those few seconds that passed, I kept my eyes fixed on the chapel. It was as unsightly as I was.

Done writing the agenda of the day on the blackboard she ordered to sit. I returned to my seat, limping as I walked.

Most heads were faced forwards, but it was obvious they were straining themselves from looking at me. I don't know if it was out of consideration or out of the feeling of comradeship, but then I didn't care since I felt none of that for other scapegoats, be it classmates or outsiders and didn't want to be a recipient of such either.

My seat was a shared space with two nice classmates and was situated right beside the window on the left side of the classroom, three rows away from the blackboard. On my seat, I stared at the chapel while trying to regain my composure in the process, but it was hard to ignore those constant but brief glances that made the tears of self-pity harder to suppress. The boys I sat with constantly asked if I was okay and I never responded.

I was obviously not okay; my back was burning, and I could feel the constant stings of the swollen lines on my calves. Everything felt so unfair, I didn't deserve any of this. I have never deserved anything and shouldn't deserve anything. All I wanted was to be left alone, to have been left alone wherever I was before being birthed.

Little by little the tears came, and when it was obvious my emotions wouldn't let me have my way, I hid my face and cried it all out. Seconds after, I felt a pair of hands stroke my back, and although it hurt, I let them be. My eyes felt heavier, so I closed them. After a wish, a hope and a few sniffs, I slept off.

I wish I never wake.
I hope she gets into trouble for beating a student to death.

DECEMBER 2013

Last month, I begged to use the housemaster's phone.

It was on a Saturday morning.
After eating breakfast, I ran to the school's music instrument's room – also the headmaster's office – and asked for a call to family. I immediately added that it was of utmost importance before he could object. He searched for my name in the logbook, dialled Father's phone on his mobile and handed it to me.

While the phone rang, I went through what I was to say and replied to the responses Father was sure to give. I felt ready and waited for the beeps to stop. Immediately he answered, I skipped the greetings and went straight to the point. *I want to go back home. It's boring here.*

It wasn't until I had uttered those words that realised how much those words had weighed on me. The phone got in contact with my tears and the tears kept flowing. Worsening the situation, my hands trembled, making nasty sounds and making the wait for Father's response unbearable. I expected Father to immediately yell at me and emphasise the purpose of this place in my life, but instead he calmly asked "why?".

To be honest, I was dumbfounded. His calm demeanour caught me off guard, so I gave a weak response. I repeated the same thing. *It's boring here.* Only then did the Father I know resurface. He first said not to be a child then proceeded to give a lecture as to why I should put up with boring things in life.

"You cannot always expect everything to be fun."
"That place will prepare you for the future...you are no longer a kid."
"You will soon come to love that place......you will come to thank me at the end of it all."

*

I might not have an end, Father. I might not live long enough to show you just how much hate I have accumulated all through these years, to show you the extent of hate I harbour towards you. I might not live to see the day when you cry, regretting your life decisions and actions. Oh Father, you have no idea how much I want you to realise that your very life principal is what makes me hate you so.

I wish there is a life after this and another after that, lives where you get to live the life I have lived.
I wish there is someone that will see to it that you experience double the pain I feel and experience triple the injustice.

These are all the things I want to say Father but what will you do when you hear this, what will you say?
Will you punish me, will you pretend like you understand me only to later yell at mom for poorly raising her kids?
Will you genuinely assure me to turn a new leaf, or do you, like I believe you do; believe your ways are just, right in all sense and exactly what is needed?

---

* Extract from Dear Father

Should I blame the old ways for making you this way, should I blame the time you grew up in, or the patriarchal society you were raised in that places you above everyone else, Mother, your kids, your peers both male and female alike?
Should I blame your individual way of thinking you are always right except those few times you openly acknowledge small mistakes in front of us?

These are all things I would like to say Father, but it isn't yet time...

Motigbo sir. I understand sir.

I waited until he ended the call before returning the phone without wiping the tears off my cheeks.

Father to say your response took me by surprise would be a blatant lie because I know you never change. Your steadfastness when it comes to my life is what has always been pulling us apart. You have indeed been made driver of my train, but you had two co drivers, Mother, and myself. Both you and society bound her hands and you threw me to the passenger seat.

Your absence gave mum more control of the wheels, but now you replaced her with some total strangers, with people just like you - unwilling to be flexible to us students, treating people like they are robots without thoughts of their own.

A WALK IN THE RAIN

Last month was my birthday, and you couldn't call cause protocols prevented you.
It made me happy.

That same morning I made a resolution, and it still stands.

TILL NEXT TIME OR NOT

MEMORY: THE SIX-YEAR-OLD

It was seven in the morning; everyone was gathered in the living room. They all had their eyes closed and said AMEN when Father, the one in the black pyjamas, paused.

They were 6 in total, four sitting and two standing. Mother sat at the very end of the living room, right next to the DVD and Wande. Father stood in the middle of the living room by the doorway leading to the rooms, toilet, and the bathroom. The doorway was to his right and Debby was to his left. The six of them made a circle.

Wande sat beside Mother and to her right was uncle, who in turn sat beside his son. His son sat beside Debby.

Debby seemed to be sweating, she was neither nervous nor hot. Her hands were on her tummy, her stomach growled, her legs looked funny, and she seemed to be gritting her teeth. Father has glared at her several times to speak louder when saying AMEN, but she couldn't help that her tummy ached. But she also knew she couldn't possibly make her fourth visit to the toilet without Father thinking she had a hidden agenda.

- A ni su 'kun eni k'eni ni'dile yii...
  We will weep no one in this household...

Amin.
Both her mouth and anus let out responses and she knew a little must have dropped on her pants. About to explode, she ran to

Mother and told her she needed to be excused. Mother asked if she had diarrhoea in a wondering tone before dismissing her.

Pressed and excused, Debby ran to the toilet and slammed the toilet door behind her without meaning to, disrupting the prayer, and calling everyone's attention.

Father's frown before resuming the prayer didn't bode well for the girl that couldn't think of anything but the severe pain in her stomach and the never-ending stool.

Minutes passed and the prayer cycle was nearing its end, starting from the eldest, Father, and ending with the youngest Wande. After the cousin finished his, it was her turn, but she still was yet to return. Father yelled to come out and she yelled back saying she was *still pooing*. Mother interrupted and ordered Wande to say hers instead.

Father's eyes remained open, fixated on the doorway beside him. Wande also kept her eyes open to look around for things to make her prayer longer and noticed Father. He was barely participating. All that could be heard from him was the sound his toes made when he cracked them.

Father cracked his toes in his usual manner, eyes focused on the path to the toilet, apparently waiting for the flushing sound that never came not even when Wande started to round up. It was at that point he lost his patience; before leaving for the doorway leading to the toilet, he asked loudly what was taking so long, interrupting the prayer.

In her rush to the toilet, she forgot to lock the door. Maybe that was a mistake, maybe if she had locked it the moment she came in, she would have escaped the dread of that morning that marked the beginning of the end, that started the rift between her and Father. Maybe being unable to barge in would have given him some time to calm down from those high grounds he placed himself on, saved him from the momentary 'loss of control'. Maybe.

Upon hearing his approaching stomps, Debby jumped down the toilet, barely managing to clean up and wash her hands before he stormed in. He took her by the wrist – almost twisting it. She screamed from the pain and instinctively tried to remove his fingers as he pulled her out, but her little hands couldn't accomplish a thing. So she kept on yelling, thinking the presence of outsiders would hinder him from acting per usual.

- Darling!!!

Mother screamed – a response to her six-year-old's cry for help. She hurried to her feet, ready to head for the toilet when she saw her husband come in with her daughter behind him, barely walking and trousers half-way up. He dragged her into the living room and slapped her to the floor.

> Igba ti aa n gbadura, lo to mo pe o fe lo yagbe. Ki lo
> maa n she iwo omo yii...ki lo maa n she e.
> Iwo naa ni every time, iwo yii naa ni...
> *Why did you decide to use the toilet when we're*
> *praying. What is wrong with you this child...what is*
> *wrong with you.*
> *Every time it's you, it's always you...*

He kept on slapping her as he talked. Mother's words didn't get through to him, but how were they going to.

- Darling emi ni mo so fun pe o le lo, e fi si le.
 Darling, I was the one that gave her permission to,
 leave her be.

- Iyen o wa mean pe ko duro paa si 'be yen
 Well that doesn't mean she should stay there forever.

He had a reply for everything she said, and when he got tired of her remarks, he shut her up with the usual "and that is why you are the one ruining the kids". Mother kept quiet and so did Uncle – Father was resolute on his decision and actions.

The sounds of slaps filled the room. The cousin looked surprised, Wande was scared and went to Mother. Mother bent her head in defeat, Uncle resumed his futile efforts and kept on saying to stop, saying it was enough. But Father continued. He refused to let her be, not until he had enough.

Satisfied, he turned to leave.
But before vanishing into the passage he left her with a

punishment. She was to kneel with her hands up and keep her eyes closed until he released her.

Unable to see a thing, Debby was blind to her surroundings. She was left curious as to what faces the four left in the living room were making, as to what tales this incident will come to be, as to what everyone else thought of the whole. The biggest puzzle to her was what she did wrong, what went wrong. It went all too fast for her to comprehend and the silence around her was no help.

Finally, someone moved. Mother approached her, left a remark, and went her way. Then the silence resumed.

With Mother's words echoing in her head, she questioned why she had to go through that morning and blamed herself for being a spectacle of disgrace. If everyone else could proclaim their love for their parents then they couldn't possibly have been treated like this, she thought. Only if she could leave this fastidiousness behind her. Only if she wasn't their child, only if she wasn't born in the first place, maybe things would have been different. Maybe then, maybe, just maybe this morning would never have occurred. The tears came dropping.

That day she realised for the first time how painful it is to live. But Father's actions weren't the main reason for this realisation. The final blow was Mother's words. Just one sentence was enough to plunge her into despair.

A WALK IN THE RAIN

"She o ye ki iwo naa pe to yen ni"?
Should you also have stayed as long as you did?

*

>I breathe and I have organs,
>I bleed so I have blood.
>I think I have my own thoughts.
>I am bred so I have my own parents
>What am I?
>
>I'm human.

---

* Extract from the poem A.W.I.R

SEPTEMBER 2013

On the night of my arrival,
a classmate of my older cousin – I was supposed to live with and attend this school with – in JSS3 offered to help. But of course, I refused. Being with her was sure to remind me of how I get to live here and not with my cousin. But despite my obvious disapproval she gave a tour anyway.

The hostel has three enclosed bathrooms - without curtains - and three toilets arranged in a row right beside the bathrooms, each separated by a wall. Infront of the bathrooms and toilets was a passageway that, according to her, most end up bathing in.

I now know it is their way of reminding themselves of the little time they had. It is their trick to get extra scoops of water from those that had some left.

Continuing the tour, she blabbered on as to how much stress those without water go through every morning and warned to always protect my water. Barely 20 minutes in and I was convinced Father wasted his money.

After leaving the bathrooms, we proceeded to the field. The field was the only open space in the hostel, and its function is to provide an area for sun drying washed clothes. According to her, the hostel's reverend sister in the convent right beside our hostel constantly checks if clothes are spread on days they shouldn't. Living in a two-story building, they could easily see over the poorly erected fences.

'Anyone with their clothes on the lines on Mondays and Wednesdays were to be punished', she said, mimicking the reverend sister's voice.

It was the first Sunday before school, every hostellite had just resumed, so no one had their clothes out and the field was empty. The only noticeable object was a huge black plastic water barrel that was obviously used to retain water from the rain. It was placed right below a dent from the roof.

The field was a square area surrounded by two poorly erected fences on both sides – forming a figure 7, separating the hostel first from the convent to the right, then from the external taps and tanks to the left of the convent. The hostel's own tap is rarely accessible and is turned off from the power source, so all hostellites mostly have to use the external taps after school from 16:00 – 18:00p.m or 18:30 – 19:00p.m.

The dormitory is separated from the field and the bathroom building via the aisles. The aisles form an L-shape, and the fences a 7-figure. Within it is the field.

We moved on to the last part of the tour, the dorm. A few newcomers – most of them being juniors – were still busy unpacking their provisions from their travel bags to their undressed mattresses, while muffling some sniffles and hiding their faces. There were others that moved on with life and arranged their supplies like they had lived here their whole lives.

The senior touring me showed me where my positionings were to be for the next three years. She explained where my wardrobe and bunk were and why.

Juniors get a lower bunk and a lower wardrobe. Mine are situated below my 'sure to become school mother' as she called it. She added on saying the positioning was probably random, laying emphasis on 'probably'. Making it seem like things were arranged to be as they were for my sake.

Concluding the tour, she moved closer, lowered herself to my height, and said nonsense before taking off.
"You might actually come to like it here", what was that supposed to mean? It was obvious we were bound to become enemies.

By my bed, I looked at the mattresses on the upper bunks and imitated them. They all had white sheets on, and their blankets were neatly folded on the lower side of their beds. I proceeded with sorting out my provisions and was done in minutes.

Oblivious of what to do next I sat still and observed my new surroundings. It was dirty with dust everywhere, crowdy and loud. Not to mention, there were a few holes in the floor exposing the bare ground. That was all I needed to hate the place.

Curious, I went out to check if Mother was still around and there she was. I found her talking with the headmistress by the refectory, her face seemed very expressive, so I moved closer to hear what their chat was all about. Although they spoke in

Mother's language and I could barely understand what they said, Mother's familiar facial expressions gave it all out.

She was putting me in the 'capable hands' of our fragile headmistress. Hands that I could break if I really tried.

Tired of waiting, I moved closer, close enough for them to conclude their discussion. Mother, upon making eye contact, put an end to their discussion and excused herself. Mum asked if I felt settled while closing the gap between us.

> *Mommy, why am I here?*

It seemed like she expected more, but I thought of leaving it there.

- It's a good school, you will come to like it.

I was, at that point, tired of hearing those words. But mother waited and that was enough for me to know her stand on the whole. We remained still for a while until she turned to leave.

Two waves of goodbye and that was it.

I returned to the hostel after watching mother's car leave the main gates. Right in front of the hostel were busy hostilities taking turns to iron their uniform on the wooden table by the veranda. Most of them looked as excited as I did before realising that I was to study as an hostellite just a month ago, before the summer school. They all seemed busy, and I couldn't understand what was worth being busy about.

Inside were some newcomers, still busy with their arrangements. They were most likely the cry-babies I saw earlier on.

Already in my nightwear, I readied myself for bed and placed my slippers under my bunk, safe from the turmoil. The new mattress felt harder than my usual, as it was totally covered in mackintosh, but I preferred it to having sun-dry the mattress every week.

Till date I have no idea why she did it, but instead of using the ladder made for that sole purpose, she chose to use my bed as her foothold with her shoes on, soiling my sheets.

One. two. three.

I waited three seconds, telling myself it was okay if she didn't exceed that time limit, but her slippers only sunk deeper into my mattress. It was obvious from her leg movements that she was sorting out her things and planned to remain in that position a long time.

I reached for my slippers, got off my bed and asked, as politely as I could, for her *to take her dirty, muddy and soiled slippers off my sheets.* But she chose to ignore me. So I thought to leave her with a warning. I did what I did best and bit her, thinking she'd simply back off and apologise. But I was wrong, as wrong as I had been the entire month.
She chose to retaliate.

From the impact of the pain, she jumped down.

With a single glare from her I felt overpowered, but refused to show it. I awaited her next action and prepared myself for anything. I thought it was, at worst, going to end with a hit on the face. One second, two seconds, after the third I expected something, anything, but I got nothing. All she did was glare and observe, which felt more insulting and belittling. It felt like she didn't think much of me, like she never saw me as a potential threat.

Slowly, her face began to lose their frowns and she approached. I naively thought of it as a good sign and let my guard down. It wasn't until I was on the ground that I knew what had hit me.

The pull was too strong for me to fight against. I let out a yell out of desperation and with that we had an audience. I scratched her and she returned the favour. She did it unfazed – without a strain. I, on the other hand, looked like I was fighting a war, at least that is how the story goes.

I refused to give in, so the squabble continued. A few seniors pushed me to my knees, and one ordered to ask for forgiveness, another whispered, "it's for your own good". She said it just like Father, both ignorant of my very best. They talked like they knew what was good for me.

To me apologising then meant acknowledging and accepting the ridiculous and childish hierarchy that exists here. So I remained quiet and the silence was not appreciated. She said to remain in that position until I was ready to apologise, and I quietly remained on my knees. But little did I know that by kneeling, I was already consenting to apologising in a foreseeable yet inevitable future.

Hours passed and we were close to being the only ones awake. My teeth marks made themselves bare under her flashlight. I wanted to stand up and run out the door behind me but to where? I was abandoned and left alone to face this fate, left alone to 'settle in'. But part of settling in includes being beneath someone both bunk wise and hierarchy-wise.

I thought the bed arrangement agreeable since I wouldn't want a foe waking up with urine on her face. But the rules of the hierarchy meant oppression, and here I am but a fresh prey. I bet I looked sumptuous with my short height and haughtiness. A once in a lifetime delectable prey.

To protect myself, I must comply to their demands. And the only person guilty of putting me in this predicament is none other than Father.

If this place is to prepare us for adulthood, then it is just to say, hierarchy and mismanagement of power prevails in the world of adult. The helpless are crushed and the ones left standing are the strong, due to either wealth, natural resilience, or perseverance. Father is proof of this; he carries his position in this hierarchy with him everywhere he goes. Be it in his marriage, fatherhood, religious stance and family, he refuses acknowledge being imperfect. His opinions and views are always right, and no one is to say otherwise.

An hour passed and my knees were giving out on me, she reminded to kneel straight. 90°. We were surely now the only ones left awake. She looked so collected as she sorted her few belongings. I turned my head to steal a glance as she, one by one, transported them to her wardrobe which was also above mine. I guess that's how things work around here.

We are about sixty-three girls living in this small space. A huge room but still smaller than the living room back home. A room with bunks one-human-body apart from another. A room with 33 bunks.

I'm sure the toilets and bathrooms are not what my parents would expect considering the money they paid, not to mention the poor history of the hostel's access to water. Weird they never insisted on seeing the conditions of where we lived.

The bathroom building consists of three WCs, three 'enclosed' bathrooms with no curtains nor doors separating them from the walk-through that has being turned into a bath place for those that don't care for privacy. Only if it was possible to use none of it.

Overwhelmed by the aches from my arms and legs, I gave in. Some minutes after I silently apologised, she let me go to bed. Feeling unapologetic, I retreated for the night with zero zeal to weep over my new life.

04:00a.m.
The next morning, I woke up from the uncomfortable wetness the mackintosh refused to allow to seep in and immediately began to clean up. I took off the bedsheet, picked up some

detergent from my cupboard and went to the field. Since it was Monday, I had to leave the washed sheet in a plastic bag till Wednesday.

Returning to my bunk with a dry bedsheet in hand, I met her awake. The smell was still prevalent in the air due to the hostel's non-existent airing system – with the doors closed – so I knew she knew. She looked down at me from the upper bunk and threatened to make me walk around the school with my bed on my head if I ever wet the bed again.

Two months have passed and despite my persistent bad habit of wetting the bed, I have never walked around the school with my bed on my head. After every incident, she made sure to ensure I washed my sheets 'before she changed her mind'. I'm sure she must have received some complaints from the other seniors about how I would never stop 'that bad habit' if she continues to be 'that lenient' with me. But as usual, life has other plans for me.

She's to graduate next year. Nothing good ever lasts.

TILL NEXT TIME OR NOT

16:00p.m.
The timekeeper rings the bell to our side of the school and the teacher rounds up for the day. One by one I watch my classmates leave the class.

Normally I would escort my seat mates to the gate and watch them walk out of sight with no fear of any consequence whatsoever – unlike me.

Some days I would listen on their conversation about that new movie they plan on buying before heading home, about the famous fish pie everyone but us, junior hostellites, has tasted. Although the seniors say the gate keeper doesn't know our faces and couldn't possibly tell the difference if we snuck out while still in our school uniforms, I fear being told on by my fellow juniors; those who like today's liars could out of spite reveal my two hostel policy violations – owning pocket money and going out of the school premises.

But feeling extremely exhausted, I followed them to the door and waved goodbye. Till they left, they never stopped asking if I felt better. And although I ignored their worries by smiling it off, because I felt even more hurt every time they asked, I appreciated their concerns. I waited until they had walked past the refectory, into the assembly ground and out of sight, before returning to our seat.

Everyone but one had left for their homes.

In front of me was a girl. She laid herself flat, butt faced upwards, on the table and I could see her thinking. She thought of how unjust life is, has been and will be. She laid with her stomach on the table and with her back exposed for the teacher to exact her authority on. By the windows were the perpetrators, they sneered as the teacher rambled on as to how, she a teacher had been maltreated by a student of her own.

She called the girl a liar, and while I silently wish the girl could have snatched the cane from the teacher and before breaking it beat the heavens out of her, I know what consequences that would have. But I sincerely wish she didn't care then. I wish she just did it anyway, unafraid of the aftermath. But like always, it is too late.

The perpetrators have had their laugh, and the girl remains on her knees, pleading on. Grovelling on her knees from chair to chair pleading endlessly for forgiveness – one that will never come. Forgiving her would bring nothing but disgrace to myself, and to forgive those who made her that way would make her a laughingstock in my eyes.

They didn't possibly believe they could use me as an item to make themselves feel fulfilled in this black hole we call hostel. Because if so, *then they better be prepared for revenge, because two can play that game.*

I talked big, but I had no idea how to get back at them. Oblivious of what to do, I left my class for the hostel. Entering the hostel, I instinctively went to my bed and laid on it with my arms helplessly stretched out, until my school mother came.

- How was school today? she asked before dropping the bag in her hand on her bed.

Close to saying the usual, a plan came to mind. I adjusted my position, sat down, and replied:

It was horrible.

When one has the upper hand in a situation, the urge to abuse that power comes naturally, especially when the power involves some kind of superiority against the majority. An unknown feeling arises making it seem like everything has fallen into place, like all remains possible. All reason is lost. The certainty that no one dares oppose one's authority is all that's left. Afterall, their titles excuse their behaviour – man of the house and the seniors in the house. I thought life easy for those belonging to these categories.

There was a time when I, like most of the junior hostellites, thought of continuing the tradition, the old ways. But then I realised that doing that makes me no different from Father, from my seniors, paradigms of what I never want to become. I thought it unfair to be treated as utilisable. I thought it wrong to create tragedies and continue a tradition I once fell victim of.

After narrating the day's nightmare of an ordeal, her expression remained unchanged. She asked if I knew the involved.

Catch one and you get the rest.

I got the name of one of the liars when the teacher reached for my legs with the cane. She couldn't help but praise the liar for revealing my true nature. I recalled the name and she asked to fetch her. I did as she ordered and returned with one on the perpetrators. She belonged to the class beside mine – JSS1y. School mother in turn ordered her to fetch the others involved. In less than a minute we had four girls standing in front of our bunk.

On my bed with one clothes hanger in each hand, she ordered the perpetrators to kneel. A junior as the liar and two seniors from SS1 as the supporters. It all felt so natural, so crude… tacky.

They, who brought me so much harm and pain, were in fact weak. They were just like every other person in here; they bowed in the face of real power, they cowered. We were no different from each other, yet they thought nothing of causing me harm, and for what? Self-appraisal, self-accomplishment?

I took the front row seat on my bed and watched as they bowed their head down while responding to school mother's questions. The entire interrogation didn't last long; school mother gave them the time they needed to respond while waiting for the perfect time to attack and there it was.

- …so …we said she felt sick after getting beaten by the English teacher.

The junior used we instead of I, giving out the fact that she didn't want to take the fall alone. Although the words came out of her mouth and hers alone, the idea however wasn't hers and hers alone and therefore not a fall to take alone.

- And…?
- And that she saw it happen.

She quickly pointed at me then lowered her head to avoid eye contact. It made me think:
If she didn't believe in what she spewed out, then why did others? Was her voice enough to convict me of a crime I never committed?
Was the teacher in any position to give such a verdict? Is my body at their disposal because they hold the rod and belong to the category of the power wielders – seniors?
Is this the luxury I was sent to experience in Father's stead?

These questions roamed around freely in my head until I slowly lost interest in revenge.

Although they didn't seem contrite enough, it was a waste of time to be that bothered. Watching them swim their way out of trouble by refurbishing their words made me realise how petty they were.

After the liars finished pleading their case, our bunk area became quiet. All eyes were focused on my school mother – we awaited her verdict. I already knew she had no plans of punishing the seniors, and that having them kneel was the best solace she had to offer.

After all, it's demeaning for a senior to get beaten or punished for a minor incident like this, especially if the other party is a junior. But Father never really cared about this principle. Regardless of how little the crime was, I only got a slim chance to escape punishment if someone other than Mother pleaded. Mother's pleas only made matters worse.

An apology. That was their punishment.

After they had muttered their apologies, the previous silence resumed. Everyone had their eyes on me as the lairs' apology required a response. So I gave them one.

It's all in the past.

That was partly true. After all, everything they had done so far happened in the past, I only refuse to forgive them for it. It is not until they have, with or without my involvement, paid for that past by going through the same humiliation I did and by feeling double the pain I felt, will all be forgiven.

But at the same time, a part of me just wants to let things be, to let it all slide. To forgive and forget.
To forget they made me grovel on my knees from bench to bench, seat to seat, student to student.
To forget the swollen lines on my calves that have a beating heart of their own.
To forget that even if I were to forget what they had me experience, those that witnessed it wouldn't.
To forget the girl in the class, still on her knees awaiting my forgiveness.

Then to forgive them for causing all of it. I politely decline. I refuse to be an object of ridicule both in my eyes and in the eyes of the girl that suffered it all. In my eyes, they did something hateful and deserved to be despised, but then again to hate the being and not their mannerism or behaviour is just a waste of time on my part.

Angry as I might be, I have to keep in mind that people change, I had to keep in mind that alone I was powerless; without Senior Deborah I would never have had that brief feeling of satisfaction that filled the whole of me when I saw them on their knees, when I saw the lines on their forehead that revealed their shame, when I saw that little crowd that hid by a corner to see what was happening by our bunk. But regardless of this fact I refuse to forgive. Forgiveness can only come once I can walk by and into my class without catching a glimpse of that girl still on her knees waiting for my signal to be freed.

17:18. With the liars gone, more people were observing their siesta. The evening prayer was to begin at six, so there was barely anytime left to enjoy a nap. My school mother was getting prepared for the evening, so I excused myself and left for the field with my prayer book in hand.

I walked by my class, ignoring its existence and the glare of the disgraced and shameful that had been following me ever since I stepped out of the hostel, till I walked past the class and into the field.

The harmattan breeze welcomed me to the field, relieving my face of its frowns and my chest of its burdens. I felt relief as I walked around the field. My white socks protected my legs from the slightly moist grass of yesternight's drizzle, and the flat shoes sheltered my feet from the little pebbles on the ground as I alternated from shoes to socks.

After two rotations, I left my prayer book, shoes and socks as a pile on the front corner of the backyard pavement of the chapel, before continuing my walk on the field, unafraid of the consequences of not observing my siesta.

Legs bare, I felt an even better relief with the grass beneath my feet, with the pebbles roughening my soles and the breeze chilling my bones. Walking beside me was a 7-year-old dog, my dog and my companion. I gave her ruffle before she took off. She ran and I followed.

To my left was the boy's hostel, then the convent, behind me was the chapel, to my right the forest and in front of me a fence. I ran round the field, changing the positions of my surroundings in relation to me, but of what use was that?

One round, two rounds, three. After the third I was out of breath. Yankee was gone, and I was on my knees.

No matter how much I wished for her presence, she never came. The field's open space made me feel nostalgic, slowly creating a feeling of longing. I longed for a run in the compound back home, for a run with Yankee and for a hug with her to remind me there was warmth somewhere. I always longed for the impossible.

With every tear that became visible on my house wear, I felt weaker. I felt pathetic, shameful, and filled with disgrace. The relief I thought I felt earlier on was gone, and the burden I thought I was rid of was back. My weakness laid me bare and curled me up like a hedgehog. I felt like I was in a void, one that I longed to belong in but left no place for me.

With every minute that passed, my tears felt all the more necessary, so I let them be. The lack of answers to my questions, lack of solutions to my problems kept them flowing as if sourced from a hidden well.

The wind brought message that there's a Home somewhere, a Home that thrives just as well without me in it. The grass rejected me, saying I didn't belong, reminding me of where I ought to be, Home. The home of my existence before my birth. A home that would never abandon me once I returned, and is most likely awaiting my return. A day so far but worth the wait.

The bell rang, breaking the silence of which I was embedded in. I slowly rose up, dusted off the dirt from my skirt and headed to the pile I abandoned by the chapel. Still a bit out of it, I took my prayer book, put on my socks then my shoes, before proceeding to the chapel.

Inside, I took the front row seat and watched as some rubbed their eyes while looking for where to sit, and as others rushed in with untucked shirts. It wasn't until a few had made themselves comfortable on their seats, that I slowly began to regain my composure. My body began to feel like mine, the sores of that morning began to tingle, and I felt pressed. 18:01, we were asked to rise to our feet and the chapel doors were closed.

The need to use the toilet only increased with every passing second, but I couldn't leave. I felt even more tortured as the door was just right beside me, all I had to do was go out, let it all out and hope to get pardoned, but I couldn't hope. I couldn't bring myself to imagine a scenario where I could ever be pardoned. The words of the headmaster echoed in my head, reminding me that no matter what I had to say, it would always be considered an excuse. So I held it in and withheld the urge to storm out.

We were all on our knees, so I used my heels to block out the outlet like two fingers on the exit of a hose, counting seconds as we rolled the rosary.

18:19. Eleven minutes left. I consoled myself by constantly checking how much time had passed, but that no longer had an effect. For every rosary I passed down my fingers, I lost lumps of patience. Four minutes passed and I ran out.

It all felt so surreal, all of it. From the wet skirt on my calves as I remained in my kneeling position, to the increasing circumference of the puddle of urine, then the silent squeal of my neighbour to the left. All of it felt surreal.

First was the probing eyes of those closest to me, moving from the puddle of urine on the floor to my skirt, before slowly scurrying away. Then there was the wave of information that left my row to the seniors, then to the males on the other side of the chapel. Then came the curious eyes of everyone, including the choir by the altar and the headmaster in front of it, after someone yelled "Ayo peed herself". Last was the silence that followed. All of it felt surreal. I knew I could hear, see, think, breathe, but it felt like I did none of it.

I heard their questions,
Were you asleep?
what happened?
are you okay?

I saw the little puddle of pee that stood out on the concrete as I was placed on the bench by a senior. Even the surprised look of the very headmaster I was afraid of, had me question my fears.

I questioned my actions and thought of the cause of this situation.

I found my earlier hesitations ridiculous, and I realised I was the only one who took his words seriously. But what should I have done otherwise. He said not to pee during prayers, he swore to severely punish whoever disobeyed, and most importantly, his beatings were a degree less than Father's. I was scared, so what should I have done. I had no words. The air around me was gone.

I knew the fate that laid in waiting. Everyone or at least most of those that sat there, staring at me in disbelief will come to pity the girl that peed herself. Although some might chuckle while quietly reminiscing it, they will speak no more of what happened today and will turn this incident into a taboo that no hostellite is to leak out. I will then feel some sense of obligation to appreciate their consideration.

This possible future that awaited me filled me with dread. I remained stunned. I had no words to utter, no answers to their questions and worries.

I wanted to disappear, but the ground refused to pave way for me. There was no escape.

MEMORY: THE SEPARATION

On starry nights we would stay outside till it became dark, till Mother couldn't take it anymore. Until she'd reluctantly allow her come with into the house and spend half the night sleeping beside me before stealthily carrying her out, returning her to her kennel.

Done with her meals, she would come for mine and smitten as I was, I always gave in.

I miss watching her whine to be let out the back door – after successfully receiving a chicken bone – for her greatest mission of the night; burying the bones in her secret haven. Her perfect spot was situated just beside the orange tree father planted in the garden front. The same spot she had her greatest battle – where she fought against a snake.

The nights were always blissful whenever we were together. Mother and both of my sisters watched movies while we watched the skies. Sometimes she'd leave to chase for lizards or crickets, and I'd follow her with my gaze until the skies piqued my interest again.

I remember my last night with her, we stayed in the front yard of the compound. Mother and my sisters were inside per usual. The only time I was accompanied by them was when there was no electricity, or when a few insignificant visitors come visiting, but most commonly is when father tells us stories – fantasy, history and fairytales – he heard as a kid.

Most of them were about the greedy tortoise.

That night, it was particularly chilly. The crickets couldn't be heard thanks to the Korean film my siblings and Mother watched. Their laughs could be heard miles away.
Yankee on the other hand was unbothered, her hearing skills surpassed mine and she continued her hunt. The reality of being separated from her felt sudden and painful to think about. I could barely look at her for a minute without turning away, so I kept my eyes on the stars, hoping they could provide me with solutions.

That night, I prayed to them like they could change my situation. I begged the skies to excuse my previous impertinence and answer *just this one prayer*. But the more I stared, the more certain I was of the future that awaited me.

Father made it clear before his departure that his decision was final, and that no one could change his mind. He said:
"The school had prestige, religion and whatnot, what is there not to love?"

It was a rhetorical and cruel question. It was like telling me:
"Your parents give you education, shelter, care and whatnot, what's there not lo love?"

There was so much not to love. I got to understand with time that there is very little a kid can have a say in. But while I agree with that, I still see it fit to see through any decision made on the kid's behalf, confirming if the decision made really is for the kid's own good.

Mine wasn't, but now is. I made it be.

*

I'm forced by many factors to have no say in my birth, my death.
The decision on whether to live or die lies on those who own one,
My hands are tied as I'm dragged through the market - my passage of time

Bound to my owners I await the day the chains break.

---

* Extract from the poem A.W.I.R

MEMORY: A MISTAKE ON BOTH SIDES

Mother already left for work and Father had been sleeping since breakfast, Wande was playing pretend with the number blocks, assigning them personalities while stacking them up in order, and I was bored. Father's laptop was locked and neither of us knew his password, there was no electricity either so we couldn't use the TV.

Normally on days like this, I would cycle round the compound or lie down staring at the clouds. But, oblivious to my normal, Father locked the doors, probably out of fear that we would leave the house and mingle with our not-so-refined neighbours. Not his words, but mine. His and Mother's actions suggest that that's the case.

But despite the fun I derive from climbing trees to catch the ripest and most sour mango. or from hopping down fences and watching action movies Father claims we are too young for, I preferred playing with Yankee. But Father wouldn't believe any of this even if I told him, he would respond saying "you're sure to change your mind once you get bored of playing with Yankee".

Unknown to him, with Yankee boredom is non-existent.

Fed up with the boredom, I sneaked into my parent's room and confirmed Father was heavily asleep. His snores went from high to loud.

The new clothes we hadn't tried out were displayed on the floor and his room smelt of his perfume. Mother said Father was tired from his flight and warned not to disturb, to let him sleep in peace, so I was careful with my steps.

I took a bag of cookie and went to my room. There, I brainstormed how to go out without drawing attention.

Both the back door and front door were locked, Wande was distracted by the bag of cookie and occupied with her toys in the living room, so sneaking out our room's window seemed most plausible.

I opened the windows and readied myself.
I pushed my head into the horizontally rectangular space of the window bars, hoping for it to pop out the other side without breaking any bones and succeeded, then came my arms. After that the rest was easy.

With both my arms out, I could easily pull my waist through by holding on to the bars with my hands, and wriggling my body from left to right until my entire lower body was out. Overwhelmed with the feeling of triumph, I hopped down from the window, unintentionally drawing Yankee's attention. Her bark in turn drew Wande's unwanted attention.

I stiffened.

With a cookie in hand, she looked out the window, first towards the gate then at me.

A feat like this was probably too much for her four-year-old brain to comprehend, I thought to myself as I drew Yankee closer. I sat down.

While petting Yankee I blankly stared at Wande, hoping to find a way to ward her off.

- How did you get out?
 I squeezed my body through the bars, bet you can't do it!

Feeling challenged, she tried coming out with her legs and when that didn't work, she tried going arms first. After successfully getting her right arm out, she proceeded with her head and the whole of her right shoulder at the same time. It was obvious she wasn't going to make it, but I kept on watching and said nothing; thinking she was sure to give up before getting stuck. But she didn't.

She looked like she was going to yell from the struggle and fear of getting stuck, so I stood up.

> *Shhh… shh, you'll wake daddy up and I'll get in trouble. If you promise to keep quiet, I'll try to help.*

She didn't listen.
Her anxiety kept her moving until she finally got stuck. It didn't take long before the tears started pouring out, transmitting her anxiety to me.

Anxious and scared of the consequences of my words and actions, I tried to climb up the wall. Jumping down was easy, but climbing back up with nothing to hold on to was hopeless. Abandoning that option, I asked her to promise to keep calm while I searched for a ladder. She begged for me to stay, so I promised *I'd be back shortly*.

Afraid of waking Father up, I lightly jogged past the toilet and bathroom windows then past Father's room to the garden hoping to find the ladder laying somewhere, forgetting that my little hands wouldn't be able to carry it anyway even if I were to find it. Minutes passed and despite my effort I found nothing. I began to lose hope in the duration of my sister's patience and in finding a solution. With that, the fear of getting into trouble only grew, so I settled for another plan – to instruct her.

I hurried back to the window of our room and found her sniffing some tears back in. It was obvious frustration was just a mistake away for both of us.

Look at me, just pull your head back like this.
I slightly tilted my head to the right and pretended my left hand was holding one of the bars and showed how to use the strength from her left hand to pull her head back in. I tried to convince her that the pain would be brief, and that it was worth it since she would be free.

- But it hurts, I don't want to! She cried almost yelling.
  Just try, it'll just sting just a teensy-weeny bit.

- No! she cried out decisively, causing Yankee to bark, loud enough for our neighbours two houses away to hear.

Her words irritated me, and I foolishly let it influence my words. *I never told you to do it in the first place, so if I get in trouble because of your stupidity, I'll…*
I'll hate you.

With that sentence Wande started bawling. She flayed her left arm that was free and hit the bars then the walls – heightening the pain her body initially felt from being stiff.

Rather than being worried about her, I was afraid. I was certain the noise had reached Father, and that certainty left me motionless. I could hear trouble coming. I heard the sound Father's door made against the wall as it opened. I knew he was obviously annoyed his sleep got interrupted.

- Ki lo maa n she eyin omo yii gan naa, he yelled as he made his way to the room.
  What is wrong with you these children, …

With his stomps nearing the room, I froze.
Everything became still. The harshness in his tone stirred the thoughts I tried to supress.

You're going to die, isn't this what you wished for? Just take it like the girl you are…
At worst you'll bleed to death…

Wande was desperate, she had been stuck for the past 10-15 minutes – head stuck outside the bars, arms aching – and was most likely scared and filled with thoughts similar to mine. Thoughts of never getting out of the bars were most likely all she thought about. The consequence of her screams didn't matter to her, just as the reasons for her screams didn't to me.

The moment she heard Father's voice, her screams intensified. She tried to speak as she cried, slurring her words.

- Daddy … help! My head is stuck and…and…and it hurts when I try to pull it out.
- Ah! Father exclaimed upon entering the room.
  How did this even happen, wait a second. Just let me …maybe if I … give me a second, I'll…I'll go get some oil.

After this, I could hear his voice fade as he called for me.

- Ayo. AYO !!!
  Ibo ni Ayo yen wa?
  Where is that Ayo?

I remained still. My eyes were fixated on the floor.

Nothing good will come out of him knowing where I was. I thought.

Sometimes I still think of some possibilities.
I consider the possibility of Wande being considerate, in her

own way, by not immediately yelling that I was the cause of the whole situation. By not calling me out and revealing my location.

Thinking back, maybe she was buying me time and expected me to run away. Maybe I should have run away the moment I heard him leave the room, maybe I could have given him time to cool down then come back later that evening after explaining, over the phone, that I, technically speaking, had nothing to do with Wande getting stuck.
Maybe, just maybe…

My mind refused to think. My mouth remained shut against or, even more likely, of my volition. I couldn't reveal where I was. My instincts compelled me to turn around and climb the gate a few steps behind me, without Father knowing my place of refuge at least not until Mother came back, but my doubt hindered me from following it through. I doubted what Mother's presence could change and I unconsciously concluded that the answer was nothing.

Father's voice felt closer and got louder, and I completely froze both inside and out.

- So, ibeyen lo wa. Kilode ti o fi da mi loun igba ti mo pe e. Ab'oro wa ba loro e.
  So that's where you've been. Why didn't you answer when I called for you. I'm coming for you later.

Father kept on muttering to himself as he applied the oil around Wande's joints and ears. He occasionally hissed and after a while he succeeded.

Done, Father asked if she was uncomfortable, and I presume Wande shook her head in response. He left with Wande and after a minute or two I could hear the front door open.

He came for me, just like he had promised.

Slowly… breathe in, breathe out … don't tremble.
It might hurt…it will hurt but don't cry, face it and deal with it.
If you die……you die, it might not hurt since you prayed.
Calm down, … now breathe.
It's okay.

I heard the front door open; I questioned my reasons for coming out in the first place. I questioned if it was worth it. But I didn't know when Father was going to wake up and I really wanted to play with Yankee, I wanted to hang out with her like I did when he wasn't at home.

I heard Father's steps get closer.
I hoped he would let this slide, say it was a five-year-old finally acting her age and tell not to do that again. I clenched my fists hoping this would be the case, promising myself I would yell and make a fuss if it wasn't.

I couldn't hear anything;
I could hear something, but it was the sound of my right ear ringing. I closed my eyes, tensed my muscles and readied myself for the next hit. Instinctively, I lowered my head, till my jaw rested on my chest. I begged my eyes not to bail on me, held back the tears as much as I could, swallowed down the bitterness that climbed up my throat. I knew that if I cried, Father would yell to stop and order to think of my wrongdoings instead.

Two. three.
After two more slaps, my head felt heavier, my ears were hot, and my nose stung. The sting reached my forehead, spreading its headache all over my cranium.

- Tele mi.
  Follow me.

I was certain I had it in for me. If I rebelled and remained put Father was sure to get angrier, then maybe my punishment would have increased. But if I heeded and followed, he was sure to punish me anyway.
I chose the better of the two.

Father walked past Yankee, ignoring her barks and proceeded to the front door, taking gigantic steps. I followed him, walking as fast as I could. My body felt lighter and lighter as we approached the door, and I sometimes had to jog to catch up. The dizziness constantly came, but I refused to give in.

But now, looking back, maybe I should have given in.
Maybe I should have fainted.

Maybe if I did, I could have changed the course of events that resulted from our carelessness that day. Maybe I could have prevented similar things from happening. Maybe the sight of his fainted five-year-old would have shown him what it means to be a parent, what it meant to be my father.
But as usual those thoughts escape me when in the moment.

With each step he took, the anger in me took a step further. I slowly accumulated different emotions – anger, spite, hatred, disgust, regret and much more.
I walked behind him, sometimes looking up to catch a glimpse of his back only to look down again unable to understand the creature that stood in front of me, unable to fathom what thoughts went through his head.

Then, I was slightly curious as to if he was going through the sequence of punishment, he was to give me while, in his head, patting himself on the back for being a good father. I wonder if he had to reassure himself that his next action was the right one to take as a parent, as a father to a five and a four-year old.

I felt apologetic and regretful for what happened. Even though I was convinced that I wasn't the cause of what happened, I was sure to never repeat it again. Then, I hoped that if I told Father of my regrets, he would let me off with a warning, and act like the father I wish I had, so I prepared in advance.

I'm sorry, I didn't know she'd hurt herself, I'm at fault and I know it, so please don't make it hurt. Would you hear me out, if I try to explain, would you listen calmly, do you have that patience or are you engulfed in your anger?
What is it you want from me, would beating me calm your anger and erase what I've done?

These words laid waiting at the tip of my tongue, preparing themselves for the big reveal, the moment of truth, the signal that would set them free and convict me of my crimes. But from the fear of cursing him out in the process, I swallowed them down.

I accepted defeat. A part of me called me weak, disgusting, stupid and foolish for going along with this life I've been presented with since I came to existence, for going with the flow. For not thoroughly thinking through the reason of my existence, my purpose in life.
The how and why I came to be.

Say it you lowlife, just say it.
Try unleashing your anger, do it. You'll regret it if you don't. Just look at your dog frantically barking but unable to change your fate. No one will protect you, no one can. You don't need protection and even if you did, you don't deserve one. You know what will happen once you go in. Turn back and run, run in front of a car, offer your flesh to traffickers, anything, just flee!

I squinted my eyes and chased away these thoughts. I shrugged off the feeling of giving up and continued following. I wanted to stall but I knew that was out of my control. The tempo of everything was decided by Father's gigantic steps.
Barely two minutes had passed since the last two slaps, but it felt like I had spent an eternity hoping for the impossible.

Father opened the door, and I followed behind him.
Yet another thing I wish I had done differently. But I was weak then. Not frail but petite, young and powerless.

Father took one of the new belts Wande and I played with earlier that day, before breakfast, but forgot on the dining table and ordered to kneel.
There were no questions asked, just accusations and what he thought were rightful punishments for those accusations.

To ba she aburo le she nko.
What if you had injured your younger sister.
Afi ko ma she're ka kiri ni sha…. pelu okunrin de ni.
All you know to do is play around….and it's with males.

He had an unexplainable look on his face as he said the last sentence, before continuing with the belt. It all went per usual, hit. then talk,
hit. then talk,
hit. then silence…, until the unexpected happens, until he loses both the dissonance and melody.

I have no memory of what caused it or why he deemed it necessary or if it was a mistake, but regardless of the cause Father's leg went for my face, leading to a hit on my teeth. Mother says they were probably loose and were about to fall out anyway. But while I can see the argument in that, I nonetheless recall it as – the force from Father's legs leading to four of my frontal lower teeth falling out.

Maybe I was hysterical, or maybe the taste of blood in my mouth filled me with dread.
But whichever it was, the moment I grasped the situation and felt four teeth swimming in my mouth, I started to scream. I slightly opened my mouth to drool out the blood, allowing it to stain the orange carpet while retaining the teeth in my mouth.

Time passed and Father was still.
I spat the teeth into my left palm, clenched my fist and kept on screaming until the screams began to have skips.

From the beginning to the end, I could see Father's feet in front of me. I could see the veins in his legs. I could slowly picture how they must have moved to hit my face, but I couldn't picture what was going on in his head before that.

Although I had already fallen silent, my ears were filled with my screams. I concentrated on Father's legs since I couldn't see his face. I could see neither his facial expression, nor could I imagine what he was thinking. But I knew what I was thinking as I held my teeth in my fist. I lost four teeth at once and for what, for a sister that wasn't injured and for a Father that didn't know what it meant to be a father, how to be a parent.

Maybe it went out of hand. But even if it did Father never acknowledged that, nor did he apologise.
I doubt he even remembers.

Seconds turned to minutes.
Father left the living room and Wande approached me, but I ignored her. I stood up, fists clenched, and left for the front yard.

I headed for the little plant plot situated by the fence separating our house from our neighbours to the left and spat out the accumulated blood I had in my lower side cheeks. Yankee immediately came and licked the blood off the soil.

I didn't pull her away until she had licked it all off. Although my eyes could see, I didn't take in what I was seeing.

My gums didn't hurt but they felt numb.
I placed the tip of longue on the empty space, hovered over it, curled my tongue to gather the blood from my gum then spat it out. It was a bit red but not like the first drips I spilled on the rug.

I watched the saliva-enveloped blood fade out of sight, into the dark humus soil, watering the seeds of hatred.
I bled but didn't die.

With the show over, I stood up.
Appalled by the thought of going back into the house, I remained outside. I chose to walk around the house.

Each time I passed Father's room, I wondered if he was bothered by guilt, if he felt the least bit of regret for what happened. And if he could, to my face, apologise and acknowledge that he took it too far. But that isn't how father operates. He apologises when no one is listening. I see it as his way of relieving himself of guilt while keeping his dignity intact.

Father rarely meets me in the eye the same day he disciplines me. But then after a day or two had passed, he would act like none of it happened and compel me to smile.
When I don't, I become the unfilial child.

I remind myself of these moments by scribbling on the concrete of the house – the fence, the floor hidden underneath the rug, the walls, et cetera. Sometimes I would use stones, but more than often I would use chalks. There were two categories: gifts and punishments. Both were written in tally marks. I felt the need to remember them.

That day, I made a second tally mark p.

I never used one to cancel the other out. I merely wrote them down out of the fear of changing my mind too often. I feared growing up with the changed dad and forgetting the Father I grew up knowing as a kid, without an apology.

A WALK IN THE RAIN

Minutes passed and I continued my walk, alone, without Yankee. Each time I passed by her kennel, she raised her eyes look at me for a second or two, before lowering them again.

One more to go.
It started with one, then that one became two. I'd say *just one more*, but the ones only became more ones.

I have no memory of how long I spent walking, but I was sure lunch time was long gone. I could see the sun go down, slowly disappearing out of sight as I walked through the backyard.

Lunch time had passed, and evening was approaching.
I spent my lunch time digesting the marks of the belt, and Wande spent it hidden in the room. Father probably ate something in his room, as I didn't hear or see anyone in the kitchen throughout my walks. Although I had only eaten breakfast and was starving, I refused to go back in.

Slowly fatigue crept its way in.
Feeling weak in my legs, I sat by the veranda in the front yard. Then moments after, my upper body, waist upward, gave up on me – so I took the mat and laid on the veranda.
Last were my eyes, but I refused to close them. I couldn't.

The fatigue wasn't strong enough to shut down my thoughts.
Would there be anyone out there willing to switch places with me?
Is this something I'm supposed to get used to because many

others struggle with worse?
Am I the ungrateful one for not cherishing what I have?

I couldn't fathom why everything had to play out the way it did. *Was I supposed to see him in a good light after today?*

After that question, I asked myself:
Why me? What did I do that was so wrong?

There was no one to answer me.
I couldn't figure out what was so good about Father – he was obstinate, irrational – he listened to no one but himself, when it came to things that mattered.
I hated him, and no one could tell me otherwise.
I found no reason to like him.

Time slowly passed by as I lied on the mat. Yankee came to accompany me. Wande too. The warmth of Yankee's fur to my right and Wande's to my left slowly put those thoughts to rest.

With time, my eyes felt heavier. My decision was resolute, and I promised to forever stand by it. I repeated it over and over to myself:
I hate Father.
Father's the worst,
never like Father.
I hate Father.
Father's the...

Slowly, my words fell silent. I began to fade into my nightmares.

In my dreams the day went on, only to begin again; creating an endless loop of growing hatred that knew no bounds, shedding light on things I never understood, telling me I needn't understand them. Afterall, it wasn't worth my time.

By the time I woke up, I was on my bed with Wande by my side. Although my chest felt heavier, my head was as clear as day.

July 2014

It is astonishing how fast it takes for a human to adapt to a new environment.
The ever-increasing ease of surviving when faced with factors, either partly or completely different from what was once regarded as common, usual, and regular.

It's been exactly one year since Father made it clear what my fate for the next five years is.
While I can understand the desire for a parent to send their child to a prestigious school, I can't seem to understand how Father never checked the condition of the place he sent me to, to know if I really thrived there.
I also can't understand how he easily dismissed my words as the complaints of an ignorant kid.

He assumed whatever discomfort I felt momentary and strongly believed the expenses overweighed the shortcomings.

Whenever mother mentioned my pleas to end my boarding school sentence over the phone, Father's voice became loud, his tone changed, and he always ended the call with a hiss.
In his rants, he would mention the cost of being an hostellite, stress the honour and luxury and emphasise on the importance of its function – one I am yet to see.

It's almost as if he believes more in the school's ability to raise kids than in our relative's.

If that were the case, then he, like he has been about many other things, is wrong.

In contrast with his beliefs and claims:
Being with Yankee would continue to improve my rationale.
Being with Father only informs me of attributes, qualities and habits to avoid as an adult and as a parent.
Being controlled by the hostel has increased my contempt towards my creator.
Getting beaten because of the wrongdoings of others has driven me further away from the multitude.
Being in hostel is no different from being placed in the midst of rapists.

But more importantly is that, I will in the future thank myself for who I will come to be and not him.

...

Being beneath someone was something I never wanted to experience after leaving the house. I thought I would finally get to be my own person after moving to my cousin's, away from Father's claws. But the constant watch of the headmistresses and masters never gave me the chance. Every second of my time was everything but mine to spend. They went to helping others, doing the seniors biddings, to the schedule they had laid out for us. Siesta, study time, lunch, prayer, procession, church, chores, vigils.
The cycle never ended.

Saturdays were a breather, since we had an hour of sports. But there were some Saturdays the headmistresses and masters

couldn't help but involve themselves in. Everyone had to be doing something, being idle wasn't allowed.
But I thrived the most when I was left to rest, left alone with Yankee, when mother gave me a list of things to do, and I had the authority to decide on how to distribute them.

However, hostel changed everything.

Whatever I did had consequences – most being bad than good. Being quiet gave people reasons to make rumours about me, being active drew unwanted attention, making friends led to betrayal and assumptions that I was in a romantic relationship.

Hostel changed everything.

A year has passed, and I have no hope of ever being free of this endless loop of turbulence. On the brighter side, I've grown rigid, stiff, stoic. I have come to have attributes Father would grow to dislike, thus attributes I'm content having.

School was supposed to be educative; I was supposed to go home and have a laugh with Yankee after telling her of the day's events. I wasn't sent there to do chores for others.

I never wanted to be ridiculed for being a bed-wetter by discontent seniors nor did I wish not to live in fear of being late for anything.
I wasn't sent here to be enslaved by others, nor to be on edge, always trying to get on the good side of seniors just to have a solid support.

And if this is how the adult world is, should everything I have come to experience be justified?

Father: ...
Does that mean you as a child were raised the same way?
Does that mean that I have to look back at my life while shaking my head in regret on how things could have gone differently?
Does that explain why I have to lose a part of me after every heart-wrenching incident?

I don't think so.

*

But you know what Father ... thanks to you I have come to understand a lot.

It does not suffice to only learn from experience, adapting what is learnt to what is in front of me matters more than just releasing my load. You made me think twice of what it means to really care for someone and to claim to care for someone.

One-sidedly expressing what I claim to be care and carefully observing what it is I want to care for before expressing my care, are ultimately polar opposites. as we are.
There were times I couldn't help but share this opinion of mine with you; but I'm but a dumb kid, what could I possibly know.

You claim I'm intelligent but disregard my opinions saying it's a kid talking, oblivious of the kid's very best. It makes me

---

* Extract from Dear Father.

wonder just when I will stop being a kid, to you. when you will grow past thinking it's a kid talking. And most importantly is when you will stop thinking everything I do by default means I'm rebelling against my parents – 'because I've reached that age'...

Thanks to you I have come to realise the reality of what I once thought of as my predicament.
There is no use crying over spilled milk – what has happened has happened, the only thing I can change or influence is what comes after.
Trust no one – all males want one thing and I must protect my mind, soul and body from them, excluding family.
My status as a child is no different from a slave's and I am nothing but an investment,
Being older does not mean I'm all that it, in fact it means whatever I say is the teenager in me acting up.
Respect is to be earned regardless of status. Your title as my father never meant you knew better or deserved better, and your actions tell me you are not worthy of my respect.
Being raped or molested does not mean it's the end of the world. Afterall, there are others out there without shelter, starving, homeless living every day without knowing what tomorrow holds.

Father I could go on and on as to how much I have come to understand from observing you, but I'd rather make you understand why I never thought well of you.
Why the emotions I feel towards you are nothing but negative

and the words I have to describe you contradicts Mother's,
yours, our family friends' and even Wande's.

Not once have you thought of your irrelevant display of
authority and your so-called disciplinarian actions as
unnecessary.
Like when Wande made a mistake and dropped your laptop
bag, you responded with a slap. She was barely five.
She might have forgotten, but I never will.

Every time I had to receive a punishment for another
hostellite's wrongdoing or inefficiency. I thought of you
Father.
Each time I got flogged for being a second late to the refectory,
chapel, or any gathering with hell canes. I thought of father.
Every time I got threatened that I would publicly be shamed
for being a bed wetter, I thought of you.

Before I knew it, the anger in me was getting wild, and wanted
to do terrible things that has already become a part of me.
We started planning, the plans were simple but mischievous –
I would stand back and watch you destroy everything. All it is
you claim to have worked hard for, including your greatest
investment ever.

M E.

This conniving part of me, I grew to love.
It helped not only calm the anger I could no longer control, but
also throw the last bit of empathy I had for you out my system.
I was grateful to it; I could finally breathe.

Father did you know it's easier to destroy than to build.
I remember most of my childhood being spent building a fortress.
I wanted a fortress strong enough to withstand the persuasions, pity, empathy, child-like love and appreciation your monetary endeavours brought with them AND your flimsy emotional presence.

I'm glad to inform you that I have succeeded. I've finally succeeded in shielding my heart and mind from being confused and transformed by you, from being persuaded.

Mother says you work really hard to pay our tuition fees and that it shows how much you love us. As a kid, I somehow managed to get fooled every time – that is, until your visits.

Whenever you visited, I found myself studying you.
I, with time, came to realise that hidden beneath your fancy perfume was the stench of exhaustion.

A sign that the slightest mistake could tick you off.

Whenever I saw how much mechanical repair you had to do on your visits that were supposed to be your vacation, I felt bad. I felt bad for refusing the life you had worked so hard to create for me and convinced myself to bear with whatever inconveniency I might have. I utilised your efforts and mustered up courage to keep my mouth shut and close my eyes whenever those consistent molesting hands of my 'uncles' tore down my innocence as a girl – I didn't want to worry mother, she had to travel for work. I couldn't tell you; you had a heavier cross to bear.

But those resolves never lasted a year,
because you visited every year.

Not one of your visits went by without you yelling, shouting, complaining, and hitting when things slightly deviate from what you'd consider proper behaviour, womanly duties, and filial obligations.

At 10 I got tired; I was tired of your flimsy attitude. Why was it always you that had to be held with care?
Why did Mother always tell us to understand your situation...and why did we have to listen when you never tried?
Why does it seem like I'm the parent and not you?

I have always told myself not to care, to remain unbothered. But I know deep down, that if I ever manage to survive and live long enough to build myself back up, I will repay you for the efforts you put in my life both financially and emotionally and I will make sure to pay you back 10 folds.

Even though, to me, this is nothing but a repetition, something I have been telling myself since the teeth incident that you probably don't remember.
I'm glad it's news to you.

There was a time when I thought it was all my fault, that I must have been the naughty one to have been punished every time you visited, but that wasn't the case, Father.

A WALK IN THE RAIN

I doubt you've ever thought through why none of your visits go by without you hitting me.

Was calling Wande a snake out of annoyance worse than breaking the smartphone you bought me out of frustration, that I got a lighter punishment for the latter?
I never understood the logic.

I have revisited my memories over and over and I am convinced of my resolve...

...

Father, did you know love kills; it scars.
With just a loss, love could make you think and do unimaginable things. At least, that's how it is for me.

Upon my return home I got to know that we had moved from the house that holds traces of our history. As if that wasn't enough, I just got to know last week Tuesday, upon my arrival, that Yankee disappeared three months ago.
Three months!!! And no one bothered to inform me.

I can guess Mother's excuse.
"I didn't want to disturb your studies".

Hypothetically speaking,
how would she have felt if no one informed her of your death; because they didn't want to disrupt her work, and since she was constantly travelling due to work, they didn't want to

cause her any inconvenience.
How would she have felt?

I know Yankee's disappearance and possible death – since she might have been eaten by those evil creatures that call themselves humans – is a consequence of Mother's and Wande's laziness, lack of attention and most importantly, the cruelty of humans.

As young as most claim me to be,
I know better than not to check if the dog is where I last saw her after shutting the gates.
I know better than to go out without kissing my dog goodbye.
And most importantly, I know better than to take a knife and kill a family member or a neighbour out of spite.

...

Hatred is what I felt upon hearing the news of Yankee's disappearance. It was directed not only at my reckless sister and Mother but also at my neighbours.

They acted like children.
NO, like imbeciles.

According to Mother, she heard from some idle observers that some of our neighbours threw stones at Yankee, even though she never provoked them. They said she remained still for a while by the gate waiting for someone to open it, until the stones increased, and she had to seek refuge elsewhere.

Oh... how the tables would have turned if I had a gun.
How could they have been so cruel to do that to a domesticated dog?

I can't believe it's the same people that, during every birthday celebration, came to our house to party and receive gifts.

Cheapskates, lowlifes, hypocrites.

It does not suffice to curse them out.
They took my only true friend and companion. A best friend of seven years, one I never said a proper goodbye to.

It hurts even more being the last to hear of her possible demise.

I .... so helpless.

Despite the unfairness those around us have shown us, I can neither avenge her nor myself.
I'm left with no one to lie beside while I cry, no one to watch the moon with while I seek refuge behind the clouds. With no one to love.

While I can love the Yankee I once knew in my heart, I can't show that love to her.
I can mourn her, but I can't avenge her.
I also know that I have traces she left behind to cherish, but I cannot create new memories, nor can I remain in her domain.

Only if I had never moved away to begin with...

I hope you are satisfied now that you have once again distanced me from happiness, Father.

...

While I do hope to see Yankee one more time and reunite with her in our afterlife, I also wish that you and I are reborn with our current roles reversed.

Only then can I attain true happiness.

MEMORY: THE PROPHET OF DOOM

As Yankee grew, she gradually became a part of me.

Whenever Yankee managed to slip out the gate, I proudly lifted her up in my arms – showcasing both my strength and our bond. It was our weekend ritual, especially on Sundays.

Before long, everyone in the neighbourhood knew me as Yankee's sister, and I quite liked the nickname.

Unlike with others; foe and friends alike, Yankee only ever made me cry once. An unfortunate incident that left a scar, but was nothing but a mistake – I cycled to fast, and she ran off course. Unlike with others, it was nothing to hold against her.

I understood her, and we shared that in common. She knew when I wanted to be alone, and I knew what she liked and disliked:
She plays only when she wants to.
She isn't to be disturbed while eating.
None other than the five of us could touch her.

Three simple rules I proudly reminded everyone of.

In our fairly quiet neighbourhood, Yankee wreaked havoc whenever she had the chance. Whenever she managed to slip out – when Mother drove out the gate.

Although she never killed their chickens nor did she injure their goats that roamed around freely in our neighbourhood, most of our neighbours thought of Yankee as a nuisance – as a hindrance to their poke-nosing when they tried to look through the gate.

They – outsiders – were interested in what went on within our fences. They would peek through the gate when Mother and Father played tennis in the front yard, and when my sisters, mainly Wande, and I played badminton.

We lived in a fairly large bungalow and our parents had the average salary. Mother worked mainly as a secretary, but also as a volleyball and badminton coach in the L.S Stadium and Father worked where he worked – abroad.
They earned enough to celebrate my birthday every year until hostel – as far as the pictures go – and made sure to invite family, friends, and sometimes our neighbours.

…

My life at our first home differs in description depending on who or what is asked.
If I were to ask the eldest and most affluential woman in the neighbourhood, she would, with all certainty, state that: all three of us sisters are overprotected.
If I asked our church members and the kids in the neighbourhood, they would say that we are having **the** life, and the pictures in the family albums would support that statement.

But, if I asked my 6-year-old self, I would have said:
I'd do anything to give it up and would stop at nothing to make it happen. But Yankee never made it possible.

Ever since day one, she made my death worth procrastinating. Every weekend I spent with her after doing my chores, increased my concealed urge to procrastinate death.
It continued that way, until I at one point wished for a natural death, a regular life like everyone else. That is, until my senses were beaten back into me.

So I compromised.
I promised to enjoy some years with her and live till I was 10. Until I reached the age of rebel Mother and Father so greatly feared and detested, thanks to the words of a wandering prophet – the explanation of many words Father hurled while he flogged.

Whenever I pressed for answers, Mother replied saying I wasn't mature enough. She'd always dismiss my curiosity saying: "there would be consequences if I told you too early".

Little did she know it was already too late from the very beginning.

It makes me wonder if things would have gone differently if she had told me while I was younger, when I could fairly distinguish right from wrong. Maybe I would have felt compelled to inform them of the constant discomfort I frequently found myself in. Or, maybe the prophecy had it all wrong to begin with.

The prophet said between the age 10 to 16,
reality said five.

During birthday parties, vigils and sleepovers Mother couldn't attend, I always ended up singled out from the crowd.
I would find myself feeling suffocated in a room, forced to watch as a familiar hand went up and down its genital until it infected my face with its smell. Although, as a kid, I never made an immediate connection between these incidents and Mother's words.

I thought of my parents' words as unnecessary, as a burden. As beside the point.
I thought: "my friends would forever remain friends, and nothing was going to change that".
I thought Mother was against me befriending a male.

I, just like those around me, merely thought of her warnings as overprotective, since males played roughly – when compared to females like Wande and the housemistress mother entrusted me with.

I thought Father just needed excuses to say something to take his mind off what he was doing while he flogged, and the words of a prophet gave him one. A strong one at that.

…

I understand that the fear of one's kid taking the wrong path is something parents have to deal with. I also understand why they'd keep those fears at the back of their mind, while making certain decisions. But I draw the line when those fears cloud their judgement. When it blinds them, excusing their actions that in the long run cause more harm than good.

But while I could draw boundaries as a kid, I couldn't get anyone to respect them. So I sought solace in a certain possibility. I knew I wasn't bound to remain a kid forever. I knew there would, one day, come a point when I'd – either through time or death – disappear from their lives.

So I said to myself:
Patience... Patience is the key.

MEMORY: A LIE OF A LIFE

Finally! He's leaving.

Mother looks sad Wande looks unhappy, Yankee's circling Father and I'm maintaining my distance from the torture of saying *we'll miss you* like I mean it.

The same cycle is repeated every year, and despite the recurrence, nothing ever changes – except for me per usual. Only the observant would notice the yearly increase in the distance between me and the love.

Yankee was always my excuse since she always circled Father. Every night before his departure, I'd shift her kennel a bit further from the car hoping the drivers never jumpstarts it to check its condition.

Morning flights, night flights, noon flights. No matter how inconvenient the time was, everyone had to be awake to say their goodbyes with a smile on. Others might have meant theirs, but I never did mine.

That morning was my last regular farewell to Father.

Wande and I woke up from Yankee's barks and the driver's knocks on the gate. Father was all dressed up, and both the living and the dining room smelt of yam and scrambled eggs. Nothing was on the table, so I knew he already had breakfast.

Pyjamas on, I greeted him *morning* on my knees. He responded asking how my night went, I said the usual.

> *It was okay.*

Getting up from my knees, our eyes met for a second before I quickly looked away.

- Lo si l'ekun fun driver.
  Go open the gate for the driver.

I nodded and left for the gate.
Yankee, like me, had a good night sleep, she also seemed as excited as I was.

It was a happy morning.
My heart was beating so fast, I feared others could hear it.

I showed the driver in and immediately took my position beside Yankee on the veranda, waiting for Father and the rest to come out.

Mother was first. She had her wig on and carried the youngest in her arms. She asked if I slept well, and I nodded. Father came out with his laptop bag in one hand and his thick denim jacket in another. He was dressed in loose dark blue jeans, white shirt and a pair of polished black shoes. Just behind him was Wande, she was also in her pyjamas.

The whole family was gathered, four in one place, two in another.

The stage was set so I set Yankee free, creating an excuse for my next station.
Free, Yankee kept on circling Father interrupting his and Mother's hugs and kisses.

It was always the same old.
Father would visit on his vacations and leave after a maximum of two months. Mother would be sad, Wande and the youngest too, and I would try my best to distance myself from them.

A hellish ritual.

...

Just the day before, Father informed me of my secondary school education. He ordered to prepare and said not to stress Mother with the preparations. I was also to promise to put on my best behaviour at our relatives'.

I took his words as a guarantee of my peace for every Christmas break that was to come. I thought of my stay at our relatives' as a peace guarantee and went along with the move.

Then, the thought of rarely seeing him was greater than my fear of leaving Yankee. A thing I, to date, regret.

...

After receiving my signal – Father's slight frown – I carried Yankee to her kennel and chained her up, stationing myself there.

I watched them hold hands, pet heads, give kisses. I watched them display love towards and receive love from a fickle man. One that to me didn't deserve the affection he received – if it was genuine. I thought it comical that they called themselves family but refused to act like one.

- Ayo, won't you greet your dad goodbye?

Up until that long vacation, I never had a perfect response. I always gave in, dragged my feet, then pinched my palms before hugging him goodbye like I meant it.

I never wanted Father to leave feeling proud of himself, to leave thinking that yet another visit peacefully went by, while patting himself on the back for another job well done, as a father.

But that day, when Mother asked me her well-charged rhetorical question, I realised that there never was a need for me to directly answer her.

Safe trip. Igbawo le'n bo.
       When will you be coming back?

I chose to be formal.
I remained where I was, spoke loud enough for him to hear and acted like I cared.

- We'll see.

Father's look showed his dissatisfaction, but he chose to leave it at that. He had a belt on, but we had a complete outsider amidst us.

When their farewells began to come to a conclusion, I left for my post and so did the others.

- Ciao.

With that, Father entered the car and Mother walked back to the door, before turning again and waving goodbye.

On my walk to the gate, I kept on muttering to myself. I couldn't help but feel repulsed by the actions of those that call themselves family but refused to listen to each other.

…

On one hand is Father, he repeatedly calls his friends out saying that in a family we should always confront one another. But at the same time, he firmly stands his ground when that very same principle should apply to him.

On the other hand, is Mother.
While I can understand why I couldn't fight back against his

obstinacy, I, both now and then, puzzle at Mother's leniency towards his stubbornness and hypocrisy.

As his pliant child I had no choice but to compliantly nod in agreement to his orders, to smile while waving him goodbye as he heads for the airport.
I had to do things I, both while and after doing them, pinch myself for – a reminder that every bit of it had to be perfect.

…

With a sigh, I closed the gates.
Mother and Wande had already headed in.

It was a sunny Saturday, minutes away from noon.
Mother was sure to take a nap with the youngest, and since the electricity was still on Wande would choose the TV.
For me, the sun provided the perfect conditions for a time out.

I released Yankee from her leash and headed to the backyard.
The trees synchronised with my breathing and the wind carried me along with its movements.

Things slowly moved back to normal.

At the back yard, I put off my shirt.
Singlets and trousers on, I laid on the floor beside the garden and watched the fleeting clouds. The trees graced me with its fallen leaves and my wounds found peace under the sun.

I laid still on the paved floor as I created memories of a nostalgic august.

August 2014

Wande's to join me in hell.

Father gave orders before he left last month, but I just got to know about it upon Wande's arrival yesternight.

Mother said to take care of her and supervise her studying for the entrance exam.
I want her to fail.

I'd rather she fails, get yelled at and punished than live six years of her life in that blackhole of a luxury.

She lacks the spine.
One strike from hell cane and she'd be on her knees.

Whenever, Mother gave her the slightest of slaps she cried. If I were to wake her from her sleep now, she's prone to yell.
I can't protect her if she cannot protect herself. There's a sequence to things.

I've tried, but my efforts have proven futile. No matter how much I deterred her from her books, she went back to them. She wasn't this stubborn before I left.

…

I can't believe Father chose to send her despite my pleas to leave. Maybe it's not so surprising, but I didn't expect him to.

I have come to realise I initially thought Father intentionally sent me to hostel because he hated me. Going by that thought, he shouldn't send Wande there.
But now that he has, I don't know what to think.

It's a jungle back there, those people would eat her alive on her first day.
But as usual I don't have a way out.

I don't think she'd want a way out.
I'm sure she's convinced by Father's words. Afterall the word 'luxury' should be appealing to kids her age, and she acts her age.

Wande's smart, but she's 'book smart'.
She learnt the 36 states and their capitals, half a year earlier than I did. She got full marks in most of her subjects, but I in half of mine.
She'd have no problem getting in.
She might even be first among all examinees in her batch.

It's worth noting, I'm not jealous this time.
I'm worried.

But as said; there's nothing I can do.

...

A WALK IN THE RAIN

She's waking up...

TILL NEXT TIME OR NOT

MEMORY: A KEY REALISATION

Ever since I left home, I woke up with regrets. Regrets that with time led to nightmares. but that day's was particularly worse.

It was exactly two weeks since we left home for school, and my entrance exam was just a day away.

I was always the first to wake up and I kept the same routine for two weeks. Every morning, my nightmares woke me up. I'd subconsciously look around, try to make out where I was, then proceed to plan my day.

The windows were always a great help.
They were thinner than those back at home and I knew my head could never have fitted in there. The window's stool was also packed, and while I did want to organise it, I was told to leave it be.

The room I stayed in had space for two beds. Ours back home had just enough space for one, a large cupboard and a built-in wardrobe for the three of us.
Similar to home, I shared the room with my elder cousin.

That morning, I woke up to no wet surprises and continued my day with my pyjamas on.

I got off my bed still shaken by my nightmare. Unable to sleep I unenthusiastically left for the bathroom.

The chores were always first on my list. They increased depending on how disturbed I was by the nightmares.
The more shaken I was, the more chores I did.

I left for the kitchen, checked the sink for plates and planned out the other chores.
I estimated a total of 15 minutes for the dishes, 7 for sweeping the floors and 5 for choosing and ironing my clothes. Washing the bathroom that early would be overdoing it, but the thought crossed my mind.

I quietly opened the back door, gathered the bowls for the dishes from the veranda and filled them up with water.
The small but wide bowl was for washing, the taller one for rinsing. The basket, with holes to sieve out the water, was used to keep the clean dishes.

Done washing the pots and plates, I poured the water into the drainage situated below the tap at the backyard and threw the food waste in the garden, spreading it out on the soil around the sugar cane. Done returning the bowls, I left for the other chores.

06:51a.m.
Done with my chores, I thought to prepare for breakfast.

Mother was asleep, and so was my aunt.
I was sure they slept off after having a good night gist. Uncle wasn't home, so Mother and aunt got to sleep together. It was a weekend.

Just like back home, our rooms were separated by a bathroom and a toilet, and opposite that was a doorway that led to the living room – a smaller and properly furnished version of ours.

07:00a.m.
Done brushing, I felt hungrier than I previously did. But with no one awake, I returned to my bed.

I tried to imagine my life in my new school, think of potential differences from primary school. Three things stuck out to me:
walking to school with my cousins,
attending masses and other catholic services,
returning to a home without Yankee.

I had too little information.
I didn't know how the school uniforms looked like; my elder cousin sad they had changed it. I didn't know my classmates to be and was yet to begin summer school. I wondered how long it would take to familiarise myself with the new faces. I thought of how much studying I needed to put aunt's and uncle's minds at ease. I had no idea what to do with my leisure hours without Yankee.

...

Time passed.
Breakfast came and after that did lunch.

My younger cousin that was to begin in the same class as I came per usual during lunch. He lived five houses away from my elder cousin's, just by the junction that led to the estate. Aunt's house was situated at the very end of the street.

After eating we studied the past questions from earlier entrance exams together. We were on the last set of questions. Year 2012.

While we did ignore exams from year 1999 and below, the questions incorporated all of our subjects from primary school. There was no end to how much studying we had to do to satisfy the adults, but most importantly ourselves. We were convinced we'd feel a great sense of achievement if we were to unlike our older cousins finish the book before the examination day.

14:23p.m.
We finished grading our last set of answers with smiles on our faces. Mine felt genuine.

The next day, I woke from the same nightmare. Although less compared to the day before, it didn't take long for my tears to wet the pillow.

My younger cousin joined us as early as 06:20a.m for morning prayer – his second of the day. After the prayer, we ate breakfast and packed lunch. After that, Mother and aunt drove us to the school – a 10-minute trek from home – both looking more worried than we did.

7'O clock.
We drove into the open parking lot situated between the front gate and a properly built building – a long block separated from the other buildings in the school. It was rectangular, long and the side facing the parking lot was painted cream yellow with a brown stripe at the very bottom.

Aunt parked the car, and we got off with our backpacks on.

The school was as big as I remembered it and so was its primary school – I had once attended for summer school – beside it. But the more we walked into it, the more different it looked.

While my cousin and I chatted our curiosity away, the adults asked a teacher and we got to confirm that there were no changes made to the agenda.
We were to be by the hall at 7:30, begin the exam at 8:00 and end at 14:00, with a 25-minute break at 10:00 and another at 12:00.

Mathematics: 2 hours
English: 1h 30 mins
GK (General knowledge): 1h 30 mins

The teacher, recognising my aunt – a mother to three excellent graduates – proceeded to show us the way to the hall before politely asking to leave.

Already by the hall, we, on orders, looked through our stationaries and assured the adults that we had everything we needed. After waving them goodbye, we proceeded to test our memory by orally questioning each other.
We were just one among many others.

Time passed and the bell rang.
Two teachers, a male and a female, came out the hall and ordered to form two lines. The girls in front of the female teacher and the boys in front of the male teacher. Both my cousin and I were closest to the door, thus first in our respective lines.

After scanning our bodies they asked for our names, checked us off the list, assigned us our respective metal number tags and released us into the hall. In the hall, we were to place our bags by the stage at the very front and find our match from the hundreds of properly distanced seats.

My cousin was four seats to my right, three seats from the wall. I was seated on the fifth row from the stage at the front – where the invigilators sat – a seat away from the window to my left.

The hall looked like a theatre hall and had 14 set of side hung windows in total – seven on each side. By the stage were bags piled on top of each other and on it were two tables and chairs for the invigilators.

10 minutes before the exam commenced, the invigilators handed out the examination question and answer sheets – no one was to open them until invigilators said to.

During the examination, I was at ease.
Most of the questions were familiar and others were fairly easy. I reminded myself, during the exam, that every effort I put into practicing and answering the questions was worth it. Every shade on the answer sheet felt fulfilling and I felt closer to freedom.

Looking back, I can see why my parents never told me I was to attend boarding school. If I had known, I would never have put any effort into studying, let alone answer the exam questions as enthusiastically as I did.

A week after the exam, the results came in.

I was in the backyard helping my eldest cousin with the pounded yam. My task was to prevent the yams from falling off the mortar.

I remember noticing Mother and aunt come out the west back door with an opened letter in Mother's left hand.
First they whispered to my elder cousin, she then whispered to her elder sister, who then whispered to her eldest brother that was pounding the yam. I chose to ignore them and continued with my task.

Done with my task, my elder cousin took over, she served everyone's portion into the different plates and her sister took it in.

I sat on the stool, closest to the veranda and observed the process, keeping in mind the different stages involved so I could actively partake in it next time. With me idle, Mother seized the opportunity to announce my results. On her cue, everyone assumed a sullen look.

Even though I was familiar with their tricks, I was worried, I was tired of trying and achieve nothing. Mother stretched out the letter and aunt said to open it. My heart raced.

I slowly took out the paper from the white envelope while repeating to myself that I tried my best. I told myself I could never be at fault if the results went awry. I thought of two possibilities:
they were either playing a joke on me or,
the teachers responsible for grading the exams ought to lose their jobs.

My heart thumped loudly.
With every heartbeat, I gulped on thin air; swallowing my spit as many times as I could to regain my composure. I tried to look collected as I opened the letter.

Two seconds into opening the white paper with some words and a few numbers, the yard fell silent. Even the crickets couldn't be heard. On the fifth second, they yelled

SURPRISE!!! Someone lifted me up and praised me for coming second of all 103 examinees.

Thanks to that, I never got to register the content of the paper, so all I have to remember my results are their words.

Although I was disappointed, I was also relieved.
I was relieved that I didn't lose my new life due to someone's stupidity, and that I got to leave a positive impression on my relatives that would come to witness more horrible parts of me moving forward. Relieved that when the moment of my death comes, I would bid them farewell on at least one positive note.

Worth noting is that it was no surprise when, just moments into this sense of relief, my hopes of peace was crushed.

Still on my eldest cousin's left shoulder, Mother mentioned my hostel sentence. I was shocked but didn't show it. I looked around to see how many of them were onboard with the plan to make a fool out of me.

There was Mother, Aunt and my eldest cousin who slowly dropped me to the ground. He gave me a few taps on the shoulder and said a lot must have changed since he left the school. My elder cousin said, a classmate of hers was an hostellite and had once – in passing – mentioned how much she loved it there. But prior to that she was lost for words and so was her elder sister. They didn't know about it.

But I had no idea what to do with that information. I neither smiled nor nodded to their attempts to cheer me up.

That night, I refused to eat dinner.
My efforts felt trite.

September 2015

It was called for.

I have lost count of the number of times she's been brought to her knees by the hell canes. I tried to remind her of what was required of her and when, but that rarely helped.

Doing her laundry on time, polishing her shoes, fetching at least two buckets of water, et cetera.
Reminding her was less than effective. What Wande needed was guidance and that required patience, but I lacked that. So I did what I had been raised to do. I did her things for her, the little things.

That was until new year.
After the Christmas break last year, Wande returned livelier than I had ever seen. I have no idea what caused it, but it has helped her mingle and make true friends.

Sure they are just as weak as she is, but she likes them and they rarely implicate her like mine did after the break, causing me to lose the only two friends that cared about me and that I cherished in return.

My youngest sister has also grown.
When we last met I quickly ran out of things to talk about and never managed to hold a five-minute conversation with her, but she seems okay. I heard from Mother, that they celebrated

her birthday in school, this June. It was quite grand; she had a
nice dress and her mates looked nice too.
A pity some of the pictures got soaked.

= seven-years apart. She must have turned five.
I'll remember to write it on the back of the picture of her
eating her birthday cake, when we next visit home.

Hell resumes next week Sunday.

Two years gone, four more to go.
OR NOT.

MEMORY: A MEMORY TO FORGET

- It was Wande.

No one believed me, but neither did I myself.
It was an obvious lie. My trousers were drenched compared to hers and Wande never once peed the bed. Or in this case, the mat.

Father looked disappointed. Mother sighed and took both me and Wande to the bathroom.

I felt ashamed of myself. I couldn't understand why I lied. Everyone knew me for it anyway, so I had no reason to.

Looking back, it could have been the fact that we were in our parents' room and not ours, the fact that I was six but still a bedwetter, that I had a younger sister and even she woke up at night to use the toilet. Or it could have been the look Father had on his face and the shame of ruining his first night back.

Later that afternoon, Mother asked us to dress up for an outing. She and Father 'had to be somewhere, so we needed to stay with Grandma for the night'.

At grandmas, we ate Mother's native food and played with some old friends we hadn't seen for months. Grandmother seemed happy with our visit.

Compared to paternal grandmother, we rarely visited her.

...

Grandma sold cigarettes, gin, beer and the like in her apartment on the ground floor of the unpainted two-story building. She had a balcony, a toilet. a bathroom and a total of 6 rooms – one of which was rented out.

There were two doors by the entrance, one on each side. To the left was the living room connected to her bedroom on the inside. To the right was the fairly large bar – as big as her living room and bedroom combined – with a large screen TV for entertainment. At the very end of the apartment, directly opposite the front door was the back door, preceded by the bathroom and toilet. The kitchen was after the bar and after that was the second bedroom with enough space for a bed for two, a medium sized cupboard and a portable wardrobe. Opposite the bedroom was the rented-out room.

More than often grandmother hired house helps to manage the customers. But there were also times Mother, a few of our elder cousins and aunts would help assist her with the bar.

...

Some of the regulars recognised Wande and I upon our visit. We weren't close but they had the habit of calling us "twins of luck". My aunts always laughed it off, and I realised, with time, that it was pointless correcting them.

On the balcony during their games, the two different sides tried to share us between themselves, asking us to choose. Those that were sure Wande had more luck than I did begged her to join them, and those that believed I was the luckier pleaded to join their team. That day was one of the few times we listened to their pleas and partook in the game.

Each day was a new game or a new strategy for the same game. It could be draughts, ludo, cards or something different. But whichever it was, they always caught my attention and sometimes left me with the desire to play. Most fascinating were the struggles of the draught pieces. They'd travel from one end to another; some die in the process while others become queens.

But more than that, were the players. I was on guard against them and was curious about them. They were weird, different and left me with questions I only asked myself:
Why do they drink so much?
If smoking is bad, why do they do it?
They aren't that well off, but spend a fortune on drinks, promising to return the next day. Why?
Why are they being so nice to Wande and me, what do they want?
Should I kill them if they make either me or Wande uncomfortable?
In that case how should I kill them?

Grandma always made sure to call us in after an hour or two had passed. She'd say:
"too much time with them and the drinks – already triple in size – could make them do things". Or something along that line.

Nighttime came and Mother returned without Father. I overheard her telling grandma that Father went on a last-minute trip to uncle's in the neighbouring state to the west, a two-hour drive from the city. After that they spoke in Mother's language, and I couldn't understand the rest.

Minutes passed and Wande fell asleep waiting. She laid peacefully on the bed beside me, torturing me with memories from that morning. Another few minutes passed, and the voices became three.

- The biggest they had was size 6.

There wasn't much I could hear after, so I was left curious.

I got out the mosquito net, adjusted it so it was properly sealed and contemplated whether to eavesdrop or not. Just as I was about to leave the bed, I heard the door handle squeak. I quickly adjusted my position and tried to look as natural as possible. I leaned on the wall, stretched my legs out on the bed before slightly placing them on top of each other.

First was the help, she had nothing in her hands. Then came Mother, she had a diaper in her left hand. She handed it to the house help before checking on Wande and adjusted the mosquito net.

- Ayo, do you want to use the toilet?

I shook my head in response.

Mother signalled to the help, and she approached me. The closer the maid got, the more thought I put into the situation. ***The diaper was for me and my lie was the cause.***

- Ayo, you need to put on the diapers.

The help's voice was gentle as she asked me to cooperate.

No, I don't want to!

I pushed her away and screamed my lungs out refusing the disgrace.

Mother asked her to stop and sat beside me.
I avoided eye contact, gathered my legs together, raised them up, leaned my back on the wall and stared at the carpet.

- Ayo... Debby.. look at me. You need to understand that this is necessary. Grandma can't sundry the bed in the yard like we do at home. It's only a one-time thing. Or do you want to continue living like this?

I shook my head in response.

- I know you don't. I know all of this will stop one day. So please hmmm, just for today.

I lowered my guard and Mother, still sitting on the bed, whispered something to the maid.

I wanted to convince myself that putting on the diaper was the right thing, but I couldn't. I knew I was the first in our family to take this long, and that in itself felt humiliating.

I closed my eyes, thinking *this too will pass*, but it was hard to let things be.
Why couldn't she trust that this night would go by without me wetting the bed?
Why couldn't I believe in myself?
Why me, why do I have to be humiliated in front of a stranger?
Why? Why me?

When the help held my hands to help me to my feet, I didn't resist. I stood up when they asked me to, raised my legs when they asked to, inserted each of them to the holes in the diaper when I was asked to but cried throughout.

Even after we were done, I kept on crying. Mother tried to console me and carried me to her thighs, but I pushed her away asking her to leave me be. I sat on the red carpet, assumed my earlier position, leaned my back on the cupboard and resumed my tears. It felt like my world came tumbling down, like all hope was lost. I knew Father had something to with the diaper and that only made me angrier.

It wasn't until my breathing got affected by my tears and it felt like my heart skipped five beats or more, that I allowed way for sleep. The tears toned down as I tried to catch my breath. But stubborn as I was, I remained on the carpet until I fell asleep, and so did Mother.

The next morning, I woke up excited to show mother the diaper. It felt like it did the night before, so I felt positive.

I peeled it off from both sides, got off the bed, put on my slippers and left for the living room screaming for mother.

Mommy, mommy. See, I didn't pee in the diaper.. See…
I spotted her by the entrance.

Mother, surprised my screams, excused herself from an early customer. She collected the soiled diaper from my hands, slightly opened it, looked at my excited face, smiled a little, wrapped it up, threw it in the bin behind the entrance door and said:

- I've seen it. Now go greet grandma.

December 2015

With the change of our reverend sister, we lost our yearly excursions. I waited a year thinking they'd bring it back, but they never did.
I only got to experience it once.

After my first excursion to a missionary and an amusement park back home, I looked forward to visiting another state, one I had never been to. But it never happened.

A week before the Christmas Carol and two weeks before the Christmas break, we'd gather by the travel bus – big enough to accommodate all 66 of us hostellites – each with a bottle of water or two and a few sachets of Nutri-C.
I remember how it felt, riding in the front seat between the driver and the reverend sister. The fun rides in the amusement park, the missionary, the restaurants, et cetera. Things I had done with my parents but don't recollect enjoying.

I wanted to experience it, at least once more, to understand why my fingers tingle when I recollect memories from that day, but Wande jinxed it. Or at least that's what it seems like.

Ever since she came last year, we never had an excursion, and the new reverend sister is yet to mention anything about it. From what I've heard there are no plans of replacement, and the tuition fees remain the same.

I doubt Father was ever informed, not like he ever bothered to check.

...

He claims money doesn't grow on trees but acts like it does.
His actions make me query his go-to proverb whenever I
subtly refuse to acknowledge something he says right off the
bat.

Ikan t'agba baa ri ni ijoko, k'omode naaga, ko le ri.
What an adult sees in sitting is off reach for a child on its toes – nothing
but a flaunt of experience.

From experience, I know how useless his experiences are. He
flaunts them around but fails to put them to good use.
He talks big but refuses to reflect on the one talking and
acknowledge how his words negate his actions.
He claims to be doing his best as a father but works towards
fathering his picture of a kid than the one he actually has. To
him no kid is noticeably different from how he was as a kid,
nor are they different from the media's portrayal of 'what kids
will become in this new era of technology and westernisation'.

Who to tell that theories and experiences are interdependent?

...

Two weeks to go before we visit Father's eldest sister – per
ritual – for the Christmas break, and a week left before our
performance by the refectory Sunday night.

This year, my class chose O come, O come, Emmanuel.
First year was the drummer boy and in JSS2 we sang and choreographed the twelve days of Christmas.

Last year we won the title "cutest group of the year" and the first-year seniors won "best choreographed". I can't say it was an exciting experience, but it left me feeling proud of my fellow hostellites. For the first time that is.

Three years to go before this sentence is over, that is, if nothing highly welcomed and desired happens.

TILL NEXT TIME OR NOT

MEMORY: ETERNAL CHAINS

- Debby, what plans do you have for your future?
  Sir?
- What do you want to be in life?
  Probably an author, an artist, or an actress, or…maybe a singer.

The yard was silent.

I blocked out the whooshes of the palm trees and longed for the familiar sound of the orange tree. I shut my eyes at the sight of the naked backyard, seeing nothing but Yankee running around in the garden. Father's silence filled me with anxiety, causing me to bore my nails into my palms, hiding them behind my back.

A bit less anxious, I opened my eyes. I watched Father's joints make familiar sounds when he cracked them as he worked on the detached generator, urging me to swallow down my nervousness. I knew I tried. I tried my best to sound as carefree and decided as I could – without coming off as disrespectful – so there was one less thing to be nervous about, but I still thought of the whole situation as nerve-wracking. There were no clear reasons for his questions and there was no point in asking them as it was too late.

…

Last year, I wrote my examination to the senior secondary one class – the junior NECO examination – keeping in mind who I had as a father.

Father wanted to raise excellent minds and he always preached about the benefits of working in a science related occupation, while stylishly condemning those who worked outside that field.

The junior NECO examination was difficult.
Particularly difficult for me because, during our study hours, I'd scribble down some ideas for a story instead of studying. There were times I managed to write 10 pages in one sitting, only to, after a week, rip them to shreds for growing out of taste.

I liked when my fellow hostellites had a read of a chapter or two. I preferred seeing them concentrate on the stories than listen to their reviews that were likely lip service to avoid "crushing the dreams of a young girl". Thanks to that sentence, I answered them arts whenever they asked for the department of my choice.

However, uncle used his connections to transfer me – with two points away from the department's eligibility – from arts to science. Although those who make the cut for the science department had the luxury of choice, I was told to stick with science.

Once, I heard of someone who went to a department imposed on him by his parents, only to, after his university graduation, return to secondary school to study in the department of his choice. At first, I thought it brilliant. I was fascinated by how moved the parents were by his passion, but then reality hit me. I realised mine were different. I understood my future was bleak as I didn't want any part in it, nor desired its longevity.

…

Barely a week had passed since Wande, and I returned from school. A different July as Father asked for us to return home for the break, as early as two weeks after our vacation, a day before his arrival.

Before that, he'd visit us at uncle's; then stay a week before taking us home. And after another week had passed, he would then travel back to uncle's, then depart from there to the airport in Lagos. A slightly comfortable arrangement.

Father cleared his throat, and I assumed the stance of obedience. I held my hands behind my back and stared at the concrete floor. The more I stared, the less I heard.

Father's lecture was hardly distinguishable from what I watched they, the tall and grown, say on TV. First was strawmanning.
He called them vocational activities, careers I could do on the side while engaging in a more lucrative business.
Then, ad hominem:
"...occupations like these need discipline. Hmmm. If one isn't careful, they'd derail and go down the wrong path. Caution is a

necessity, and you lack that; all you do is chase boys."
Last was steelmanning – Father's version:

" ...but nothing is impossible. One could become a lawyer and an actor if they know where they're coming from; keeping in mind nothing but their goal. That's all I have to say, you can go".

I left for my room, with my head held down.

To him, he might have convinced himself that he cared, that he acted like the rational Father someone had talked him into being. But to me, what he did that day just showed me what it was I was running from.

MEMORY: ANOTHER ONE

One of many, but still a first.

There are many things I want to ask the boy.
Why me?
Did I look like an easy target or was it just my turn on your list?
What provoked you to do that? If anything.

While other males in hostel tried to do what he did, all of them stopped when I yelled, or when I threatened to report them, but he continued all the same.

That day, I felt powerless, and it felt real. Ever so real compared with my experiences prior to hostel, before I began my menstruation and before I got used to being free from all sorts of unavoidable sexual molestations.

I remember taking a break from class.
It was in the afternoon; we were observing our 14:00pm break, before the obligatory 1h 30 minutes extra classes began. Normally, hostellites would eat during this period, but I felt unusually tired that day, so I went to the chapel out of habit. Normally, I'd circle the chapel until I had to return to my class, but that day the doors were open, so I went in. There, I met another hostellite; he was one of the servers I'd, once or twice, seen during the masses on Sundays.

I saw him leave for the mini sanctuary as I entered, so I thought he had a task to do.

Ignoring his presence, I moved to the row at the very far back of the church's left side, sat down and stared at the crucifix. It was fairly large – his head was bent to the left, one leg crossed over the other in an uncomfortable manner. It left me inquisitive.

What thoughts crossed his mind moments before he died?
Did he perhaps know what he was getting himself into?
Did he know that despite his death, hypocrites like Father run rampant?
He must have, right? Right?

The more I stared, the more familiar the situation felt. It was like I had spent half my life staring at something similar, as that very same thing stared me back.

The boy came out.
He was dressed in his school uniform as I was.

Getting down the altar, he casually struck a conversation with me – which I thought unusual. We were classmates but we rarely talked, both inside and outside class, since we were in different departments and hostels. He was in the arts department, and I was in the science department. He was a male, and I was a female.

We were two worlds apart so I find it difficult what could have caused it.

He talked as he shortened the distance between him and I, but I thought nothing of it. I casually responded his greetings and questions while hinting that I wanted to be left alone, by keeping my answers short. But he ignored them.

First were his hands. He placed them on my chest and I slapped them off, while glaring at him and hoping I got the message across. After that it became silent for a while, and he remained where he was. I had no plans of taking my eyes off him if he didn't walk away, so I stared into his eyes, and they in turn told me his plans. I could see that his actions were well-planned, and that he had no plans of ending his shenanigans there.

He said nothing and neither did I. I didn't want to make any rash conclusions, so I stood up, walked around him and headed for the main doors, but he held me back and drew me closer to his lips and hips. I pushed him away, but that didn't stop him. So I ran. I ran towards the door, but just as I got to the front row, he caught up.

Was I always this slow?
With that thought half-way through he pushed me down; my hands were placed behind me, gathered together in a hand, and my face was pushed towards the bench.

I scratched him and managed to free my hands, slapped him, bit him and he returned all three twofold.
I was surprised, it was like he was on something. His behaviour was alien to me as he seemed different, but I later got to know that was just him being him.

The boy continued to push me towards the bench, trying to get me in a lying position, and I focused on getting his hands off me. I had longer but blunt nails, he had shorter but sharper ones. Whenever I scratched his hands of my waist, he scratched mine back till I bled. I got tired fast and was close to panic. My pinafore was a mess, and my shirt was wet around the armpit region. It felt like I was fighting a war, one that lasted hours, but only a minute or two had passed since I ran from the back seat and my efforts seemed to be getting me nowhere.

My next hope was in screaming.
Most of the students were at the kiosk, at the other side of school, others were at the heart of the school having fun where I left them, and those that were around the chapel were too far away to hear me. The chapel was off grounds for the day students, so they kept their distance, but I screamed anyway. I screamed hoping the kitchen helps were still around after preparing lunch; they were most likely the closest.

He tried to cover my mouth, but I bit him. He slapped me and I slapped him back. My face and head hurt even more, and I felt dizzier and weaker. After an extra 30 seconds of squabbling, I found myself in the same position as I was in the beginning of my loss, at the moment of my failure.

I was left with little to no alternatives.
I felt defeated, weak, pathetic and afraid.

Weaker, my resistance made no difference this time around. He had me where he wanted. His face neared, and the distance

between his hips and mine closed. I felt the tears well up as I
felt his tongue on my neck and his breath on my face.
I wanted to vomit, but that was only the beginning.

He proceeded to pull down my underwear.
His were already lowered, so he drew close. I didn't really
understand the gravity of things until his genital came in
contact with my behind. The feeling of his flesh making way
into my genital was a lot of things but anything positive. I lost
it.

I used my back to push him to the floor and pounced on him.

Although both his trousers and my underwear were still
lowered, I didn't care. I knelt down on his arms, pinning them
down, sat on his torso and began to slap. I wanted to destroy
him, ruin his body so it was incapable of functioning. I wanted
to break his nose until it was dislocated, rip him to shreds
with my teeth, scratch his face until it was deformed, clench
my fists together and hit his chest with all my might, while
hoping he dies. But I never got to do all of it.

While I did accomplish half of my punishment for him, I still
regret being unable to finish what I had started.

I kept on punching him, on the nose until I smelt blood. I
targeted his eyes while wanting him to feel helpless, weak,
afraid and pathetic. To feel death knock on his door.
The desire to kill him clouded my ears. I could hear a voice, but
I didn't care whose it was. I kept on punching while screaming
as loud as I could, masking my tears as screams, ignoring his
desperate scratches on my legs to be set free.

A man's inquisitive voice came from the window where I first sat, he exclaimed after properly taking in the situation. I heard his desperate attempts to come in through the main doors, but, unknown to me, they were locked. I heard his keys jingle till he made his way in – he came in through the mini sacrament. I didn't stop despite hearing his nearing pleas to. He was also one of the servers, but he had a higher rank than the boy and he was much older.

The scent of blood was faint, but I remember it like it was yesterday. It filled me with the desire to make him bleed even more.

While the man lifted me up, I still continued. I kicked my legs relentlessly into the thin air. I felt crazy, but I wanted to remain that way until all I could see was the boy's unconscious body.

As he lifted me off the boy, I yelled even louder. I screamed out my dissatisfaction and held my desires secret.
Let me down!!! I said.
I want him to die. Why...why won't you let me kill him. Please, please just let me kill him. I thought.

The man helped me with my underwear and sat me down. I resorted to tears. What I felt was worse than anger. It was anger, fear, relief, sadness, pain, regrets and many more combined together. Catching a glimpse of the boy standing up, pulling up his trousers and keeping his head down, filled me with regret.

I regretted not killing him. I regretted not having targeted his puny reproductive organ, partly ruining his future. I was pained by the fact that it took me too long to fight back, sad for myself and relieved over someone other than me knowing of this incident. Someone I felt would never tell my parents, if I begged not to. Someone I, prior to that day, never conversed with, but still felt comfortable with.

The three of us remained still until I calmed down. I sniffled in the last remaining tears, took out my handkerchief from my pocket and wiped off the mess from my face.

...
One deep breath and I mustered up the courage to look them in the face. First the man. He had a worried look on his face but refrained from touching me. Then the boy. I ran out.

The main doors were still locked; I panicked. With my cheeks full, my mouth couldn't contain it anymore, so I frantically looked around for another way out – forgetting the sacrament. Upon seeing this, the man hurried to unlock the doors.

Out of the chapel, I let it all out.
I puked out my system, displaying the disgust on the grass by the veranda of the chapel, close to the stairs leading to the kitchen. I felt my stomach sting and my chest felt irritated. I hadn't eaten since breakfast at 07:00 so there wasn't much to vomit. The more I remembered, the more I tried to vomit, but

with very little to let out my stomach only hurt even more. It felt like death.

I don't remember much after that, but something I refuse to forget is seeing the boy on his knees.

I was crouched up on the veranda by the entrance to the mini sacrament when the four of them returned from the kitchen. The two kitchen helps, the man and the boy.

The kitchen helps came to beg on the boy's behalf. They informed me of his scholarship and said that the reverend fathers were the ones responsible for his fees and for caring for him; one mistake and he is out. They told me how deeply remorseful he was, but I didn't buy it.

I was yet to see the length of his remorse.
He was on his knees, head faced downwards, but that was barely enough. The ceiling of the veranda shielded him from the sun and, the light revealed the life that flowed through him. I wanted him dead.

But I couldn't.
I couldn't kill him even though I deeply wished to. I couldn't make him suffer; I couldn't do anything. I didn't want the authorities to do something either, especially not the school authorities. But that wasn't something I wanted them to know. I wanted him to live in fear, in fear of me telling on him. But I questioned how effective that was.

If he was really afraid of the authorities knowing of this, he would never have done it to begin with.

He would have stopped when I threatened to tell on him.
Or did he think I was a joke, that I secretly enjoyed it despite how hard I bit him and fought against him?
Or was it because he on the crucifix watched on even after the boy's flesh came in contact with mine?

Only if I had never attended this school to begin with, if I had just graduated with the kids from my primary school, those I was already too familiar with.
Only if...

I heard the man call my name.

- Ayo...
  Ayo...Ayomide.
  Hmm.
- Please forgive him, he has promised to never do it again.

He smacked the boy on the head before continuing.

- See...his stupidity took a hold of him. I beg you, on his behalf, hmmm......please let this slide.

I resumed my tears, a bit more silently this time. I raised my head up, tried to retain the tears and said while closing my eyes:
It's okay, I promise not to tell anyone.
For now.

- No, no .... please promise to not ever tell anyone, never ev...

A WALK IN THE RAIN

The boy moved closer, while pleading on his knees and rubbing his palms together in a hypocritical manner. But before he could finish his sentence or close the gap between us, the man slapped him.

- Sho wa okay, sha?
  Are you sure you are okay?
- A'n ba e be'be o tu'n so 'ranu.
  We are here pleading on your behalf, and here you are saying nonsense.

I loosened up a little bit.
Although I never promised to 'forever keep my mouth shut about the incident', the women thanked me, and the man helped me to the kitchen. I got some water to wash my face with and got to eat some leftovers from lunch.

The school was quiet, so I knew that classes had commenced.

During my meal, the man returned saying he had informed the nurse that I was sick and said I could rest there for the rest of the day if I wanted. I nodded my thanks, and he said his goodbyes.

- I hope you feel better. And with that he exited the kitchen.

I wonder if I can now claim that I no longer hold anything

against the boy from that day. I think I'll never know, at least not until I see him again. Maybe all I'll do is punch him in the face, or maybe I'll kick him in the crotch. Or maybe I'd, like I did after that day, ignore his existence.

It was yet another incident of rape, another nightmare, another incident that came with my existence in life, with my presence at that school, and with Father's obstinacy.

An incident I wished could have gone differently.

A WALK IN THE RAIN

July 2018

This is how it continues.

You finally said it.
The first round was a mistake, the second too. But those two mistakes were enough to continue the chain reaction. Your voice heightened before finally coming to halt, you felt relieved but anxious. Now that you've said it, what next?

Father's stomps responded:
dReAd. But you were too drunk to hear.

That day, his irrationality spilled the hatred, but he wouldn't see that. All he could see was the teenager that lashed at her mom for something he thought necessary; discipline.

The day started with a chain reaction. We knew we could stop it, but we chose not to. We let you blow off steam, and you heeded. You felt better, you called him out for his hypocrisy, Mother saw you for who you were, you felt the chains loosen, but all of it was short-lived.
Like everything else.

It all started with the pup's dung, everyone but you had seen it.

That morning, you remembered the pants you had on the cloth line and went to take them. Naked, with only a towel to hide it, you rushed past the living room, into the kitchen, out the back yard and repeated the process backwards.

A WALK IN THE RAIN

There were visitors; uncle and his friends, so you didn't want to be seen naked by Father – he was sure to complain.

Done putting on a singlet and a pair of short trousers, you heard Father yell for the three of you. You answered.

Your sisters were already there, in their school uniforms. He said to stretch out a hand, you were first.
"Everyone must have seen the dog's poop at this point, why didn't anyone clean it". You saw his eyes, they looked hideous, extraordinarily hideous and they disgusted you. You looked at the lips that uttered those words and they were no better. You spoke back.

"I was naked when I passed by and walked too fast to see anything."
He smiled; you were confused.
It seemed like he was enjoying it, and Mother, a witness to your testimony, continued with her preparations for work uninterrupted.

After the smile, you looked at Mother – resting your eyes on her. You stared at her till you knew she felt your gaze, till you were sure she meant to ignore your demanding eyes.
You were furious.

10 strikes and that was it.
Although they weren't painful anymore, your palm and fingers still felt numb.

That morning, his presence felt particularly unsettling. The more thought you put into the whole, the more you felt your stomach turn. You left for the room. Some time passed and you heard the youngest cry, she was 8. Your fury heightened.

Composed, you left the room for the backyard.
Back and forth. Back and forth.

With a calm look on your face, you paced around. Your puppy came to console you, but that was of no help. The whole of you seemed to bounce off every thought of calmness you forced upon it. Deep inside you were screaming, yelling at Father, venting out everything you bottled up within you and inside us. We banged on the door and you stood your ground. At least for a while.

Thinking you felt better and had succeeded in subsiding us, you returned indoors. Heading for the room, you saw Mother, she asked for you to help her fetch her lunch bag from the kitchen. You heeded.

Frustration crept in.
We felt it coming but never warned you. We waited until the moment you scrubbed hands with Mother, until your fingers were about to part. Exactly one centimetre apart, we ambushed.

> *If I were to talk, you'll say I'm being disrespectful, but why? Just why...why do I have to keep quiet while he rambles on as to how we misbehave when he's the epitome of misbehaviour. You'll tell me to hold it in, to understand him but I tried...I really tried. I explained my situation thinking he'll listen. Thinking he'll at least try to*

understand. But he smiled...he actually smiled. How could he even punish children leaving for school, why would he let their morning start on such a negative note when he'd hate if any of us were to disturb him or cause him inconveniences before an important outing. Why do I have to tolerate him. WHY!!!

Relief came in and frustration left us. Our hold over you loosened, and you took over. Conscious, fear crept in, but the sense of relief was so satisfactory you felt drunk. So, you continued.

Why...., just why. Why ME?
I didn't choose him, you did. Why do I have to analyse him, think of his dos and don'ts, and accept them no matter how unreasonable they are...

The little mistakes hurt, they invoke shock and your drunkenness that day was one of those little mistakes.

Shocked, you were unable to complete your sentence. You were surprised by yourself. How did you miss his footsteps, the angry stomps you heard only after the first slap, during the millisecond gap between it and the second, and those that came after. The stomps echoed in your mind as if torturing you with your forgetfulness. With your carelessness.

We were always careful, we acted with care, we'd think through every step. Analyse a situation before we acted. We thought we had long since dropped being carried away by emotions, but anger once again prevailed, and so did frustration.

The rings from your ears shook us off, the shock from your series of mistakes that morning left you stunned. By the time you regained your consciousness Mother was gone, your sisters too. Only you and Father remained in the living room, you had no idea where your uncle was. You had a faint idea where your body was.

The more you tried to look around and understand how much time had passed, the more your head hurt. Soon, you felt sore in your stomach, the back of your ears, your back, your legs, then your chest. You held the tears back.
It felt like the belt. He had a belt.

Conscious of the pain in your body, you listened on what he had to say.

He accused you of always talking 'this way' in his absence. He brought up the incident with the boy from your new school and said males were all you thought about. He accused you of getting drunk by the compliments you received from males about the small growth your body experienced. You felt defeated.

Although none of them were true, there was nothing you could do. While there was a lot you wanted to do, you couldn't possibly carry out any of them. As stubborn as you were, as selfish as we claim to be, we couldn't bear to kill him. Even though Mother also had a hand in that day's chain reaction, we couldn't afford to shoulder the burden his death would put on her.

Done, but looking even more furious than you had ever seen him. He yelled to kneel and raise your hands, you obeyed.

We assured you that this suffering would serve as another foothold of our promise to you. Forgiving Father was out of the question, and our already full-to-the-brim hatred has finally spilled. All that remains now is patience to tilt the bowl till it topples over. People will call us names; some will say we are unfilial and others could call us rebels. But what they say can have no effect on us, we couldn't care less.

He has earned what is coming for him and you have learnt who you are.

MEMORY: 17 MAY. 17

Two months left.
Nearing the end of my first year in senior secondary school, I was asked to join more clubs for extracurricular activities. Left with no choice but to succumb, I joined the Red Cross, the drama club, the sports club and the YCS (Youth Catholic Students). The more I joined the lesser people I needed to familiarise myself with. At least that was what I initially thought.

Barely a month into YCS and having only been to their meeting once, I was asked to go on an excursion trip with them to the headquarters for their annual election. The thought of an excursion intrigued me, so I consented to it.

We were to depart after school on Friday and return home Sunday afternoon. My elder cousin helped me pack that Friday morning. She placed my books in her school bag, and I put my necessities for the trip in mine.

An hour after we left school, the bus made its way into the compound. We were 25 in total.
Something felt different from the missionary we went to in my first year, but I couldn't point out exactly what. Regardless, the trip, in general, felt vivid and more substantial than the missionary excursion in my memories.

18:35.
We entered the reception – first building from the gate – and waited for instructions regarding our rooms. Most of the girls were from my class so I was at ease. I had planned precautions to avoid revealing my secret to everyone and felt more assured.

In the reception, a teacher handed out pamphlets with the planned-out agenda. The official agenda was set to begin after Friday's dinner. Saturday included a few activities with all of the different schools interacting together – football on the field, after-election party in the hall, et cetera. Sunday included only a morning prayer at 06:30 and breakfast at 07:00. It was like hostel but with a different theme.

After choosing a bed from one of the upper bunks I colonised it with my bed sheet, pillowcase, a thin blanket and my almost empty backpack. Curious about the other parts of the missionary, I walked around.

Coming in was the gate, then the reception in the same building as our dorms – a long stretched out building – and opposite that was the chapel, same size as hostel's, but differently built; the veranda was smaller.

After our dorm, was the refectory. It was another building on its own, located right behind the dormitory building. Beside that was the reverend fathers' quarters. Unlike the dorm, it was a one-story building – spacious, with some sparsely arranged shrubs. Reaching a dead end – as the footpath came to a curve – I chose to explore the quarters.

A WALK IN THE RAIN

The reverend fathers' quarters had two cages with two dogs. One was hostile and the other wasn't. As I approached them, the brown one kept on barking and the black dog never bothered to look my way, but I wanted to pat her anyway. Upon patting its head, it looked at me before proceeding to lean its head towards my hand. It was bigger and fluffier than Yankee but cute all the same. I assumed it was a female, because Yankee was one, and decided to settle there.

The quarters was quiet.
I saw people with different uniforms pass by; some I recognised from the inter-school competition last April, some I didn't. I counted a total of five different school uniforms, excluding ours.

Some minutes passed and my female classmates came to fetch me. They wanted to go to the boys' dormitory and since I was yet to explore that area, I followed.

Dinner came and after that did the evening prayer. The prayer took less time than I thought, but it could have been my absent mindedness at work.

After the evening prayer I retired to my bed. I hadn't touched water, not since we left school and felt positive about the night. The voices of the girls, both familiar and alien, was the last thing I remembered from that night. The lively chatter that seemed to last an eternity; one I couldn't bring myself to enjoy.

- Make our school proud.

I took these words seriously and began to list out things I thought would benefit the association. I spoke freely during my propaganda, but it felt more articulated and planned than I had intended.

As the president I'll be sure to be transparent with the process we'll go through as a board in this association…
This position comes with great power and with great power comes great responsibility. I can confidently assure you, dear ladies and gentlemen, that I would be the responsible and capable president this association needs. Thank you.

The hall echoed with applauses.
My classmates seemed happy, my teachers welcomed me back to my seat with smiles on their faces. It felt quite exhilarating hearing murmur-like compliments from strangers.

The voting process for presidency commenced. We, the candidates, were called up on stage – there were only two of us. We were asked to turn around – backs against the ballot box and the public.

Familiar steps approached and receded. My heart raced. I told myself to cherish the moment, that it was more precious than winning the post since I initially had no intention of winning. Some minutes passed and the votes came out – I was 7 votes behind my opponent. It was expected as I joined last minute anyway. But with no candidate for the position of vice-president I was next in line. The panel of judges asked the public if they were in terms with me being vice-president. They yelled as one; YES!

I was ecstatic and returned to my seat with a slight smile on my face. After the election, my mates congratulated me and I thanked them. A teacher from my school hugged me and I didn't push them. It was quite a happy memory.

Done, I took a walk by the field. The boys were preparing for their football match. It was noisy, but it felt like the right atmosphere to be in. On my walk, a few strangers came to congratulate me, and I smiled them away.

I spent my time on the walk picturing the meetings I would soon have to attend, thinking about things that would soon come to matter. I could see myself slowly working my way up to the position I never got. Travelling to Rome to talk with actors of importance. Prior to that day, I couldn't see myself becoming something other than what Father had in mind. I was happy with my decision.

During dinner, I took my first steps.
Done with my food, I left my table in search of the new president. He told me he was just as clueless as I was on the next course of action, so I abandoned the idea and moved on.

I checked my wristwatch. 18:45 pm.
Dinner's an hour earlier compared to hostel.

With an hour to spare before the after-party. I left for the dog cage.

She was resting. She seemed more peaceful than the previous evening, so I sat even closer to her cage with my hands on her back. Out of habit, I mildly stroked her, back and forth, forth and back.

The stars shone bright that night, it almost felt unnatural. I looked up, stretched out my right hand and scanned it with the starlight. The day felt like a dream, but I knew better that to think it was a dream. My dreams were chaotic; they felt like simulations. I was always trapped in a familiar yet unfamiliar location constantly trying to get there with no idea where. I wake up wishing to be somewhere I believe as my final destination, left with unfathomable feelings of longing.
I felt all over the place.
What do I want?
Can I get what I want?
Should I live how I want?

What do you think Yankee.

July 2017

He did it again.
After our talk about my future plans yesterday, he had a talk with Mother.

According to him, being away from home for too long could be damaging. So he said to move in with Mother. "It was in our best interest".

It could be because I told Mother I never wanted to marry and would rather become a nun.
I blame my naivety and lack of patience when Mother prods on my involvement with males.

They've given us a false sense of free will; they told Wande and me to choose a school of our choice but I know very well that they'd never settle with our choice; if it meant we'd have to transport ourselves there via public transport.
Mother said to first choose a secondary school for the vacation and then see if we'd want to continue there for the rest of the year.

I have a faint idea of what to choose. But I'm tired.
With Father, it's one thing after the other.

I feel like I betrayed my mates from SACHS, leaving them with the title of losing a post only two months in. I knew I never should have gotten involved. I never wanted to get involved anyway. My involvement in life has always brought me nothing but harm, shame, disgrace and disappointment.

I acknowledge that I had my hopes up, that I, for once in my life, believed I could lead a life of my choice.
I acknowledge that I deviated from who I had promised to be.

I also acknowledge that once again, you were right, and I was wrong.

I think it's about time I put an end to this façade.

TILL NEXT TIME OR NOT

A WALK IN THE RAIN

Good morning. My name is Ayomide.
I'm 13 and will be turning 14 this November. Nice meeting you.

I slightly bowed my head signifying the end of my presentation. The 5 of them clapped in response.

There were six chairs in total and only one was unoccupied. It was a small classroom with few students compared to SACHS and the school I attended for summer school. The classroom was on the second floor of the three-story building and my chair was situated beside the window on the east side of the school. Beside me was a bungalow, it resembled our home.

First class of the session, 8 in the morning. The view of the neighbouring house was all I could see for weeks.

The class was only big enough to accommodate 15 seats and there was a blackboard. I felt out of place. My mind was clouded with thoughts I couldn't put to words. Not to mention, I disliked the unfamiliar atmosphere and felt choked with the differences.

In comparison to this, my first day in SACHS was peaceful. My classmates knew me for being on my own. They were younger then and thought nothing of it, they grew to know me for it. The familiarity I felt with them was convenient and I missed it.

I pondered on how long it would take for my new classmates to understand how I wanted to be treated, but I couldn't be bothered to put any effort into it either. I knew it wouldn't last forever. Two years of secondary school and we'd go our separate ways, they to theirs and me to mine, that is, if I lasted that long.

They were outgoing. Two weeks into the term and it felt like they knew everything my mates from SACHS knew about me. We had talked about family – the basics. We talked about our past experience in school – the insignificants. And had discussed our dreams; without prying too much or asking too little. There was a hint of satisfactory balance just two weeks in, and it felt weird.

My grades on the entrance examination made little impression on my new teachers, but my little but significant engagement in class ruined it and so did Wande's improving assessment skills. But I learned to live with it, as I did other things. The more attention I got, the less involved I was in school.

With time, I was left alone whenever I went to the quiet room.

On the third floor, at the left corner of the school – right behind the school hall – was an empty class with only three chairs in it. No one, but me, went there during school. I enjoyed my stays there as it gave an even better view of the neighbouring house, and I enjoyed the silence that part of the school had to offer.

But after a few months, we became two. Same time, every Tuesdays and Fridays, the mathematics teacher of the third junior year would come in with a delinquent, asking me to make sure he studies – something I never bothered myself with.

There came a time when I thought it intentional, but there was no reason for me to voice it out. While he did talk a lot, despite my indifference, he respected my boundaries and never inquired what I worked on in my book.

Time passed and we'd walk home together. We lived on the same street, so I let him be.

Six months in, the teachers noticed a pattern in my grades and called me for counselling. They asked if I was dissatisfied with my department, and I said *I don't know,* as politely as I could. While I did want to change to a department without chemistry in it, saying that will be overdoing it, so I let them do the needful in my stead – plead on my behalf.

With some convincing words from the principal, mother agreed to changing my department. She asked for the best option, and they said social science; reason being arts had three unfamiliar courses compared to social science like French,

CRS and Literature; subjects I hadn't done since JSS3. Mother agreed.

I have no idea if she informed Father before she made her decision, but it never mattered.

MEMORY: OUR DEMONS

I just can't picture it.
I'm a hundred percent certain I'll open my eyes during a kiss.

It was quiet for a while, until someone giggled. Then came another and after that came a few more.
I didn't understand what was funny.

I think we were about nine that day.
We were in front of the school gate, about to say our farewells until someone brought up the topic of an ideal kiss.

It started with the fascination of feeling immersed, a feeling that could according to six only come if the eyes were closed, then escalated to the different types of kisses as the discussion heightened – voices overriding one another – and got off course, entering the spicy zone. Wande wasn't there so it felt less awkward.

I watched them talk with fire in their eyes, it was intriguing – at least for a while. While they talked, I told myself not to get involved, but the more I listened on their respective takes on the matter the wiser I thought it was to show them the differences between us.

As of the time, I couldn't picture a scene where I'd voluntarily kiss someone and it was something I took pride in, thus something I wanted those around me to know.

During the giggles, Wande and my youngest sister came out and the discussion came to a conclusion. We then dispersed and went our separate ways. I left thinking I could never change my opinion on that matter. I couldn't picture why.

That was before I knew him, after I met him.
The more I saw him, the more time I spent with him, the more I thought about him.

I think our first kiss was in the quiet room, a week or two after the Christmas break in January. I closed my eyes for a minimum of four seconds before opening them back from the thought of eating him whole.

I warned myself and told myself to stop before it got too late, to heed my fears and pay my past notice. I knew what it meant to get involved with life, so I warned myself.

Life is nothing but a façade. I need to remember that.

NOVEMBER 2018
"DON'T TEXT ME ON FB ANYMORE"
"COULD YOU COME OVER?"

I messed up...
But he messed up even more...

I knew Father surveilled everything I did on Facebook and even edged him on. But since he and I barely used it, I thought it unnecessary to tell him the reason why. All I said was to never message me on the platform.
Should I have told him?

Hi, my father looks at my chatlogs on all my social media platforms except WhatsApp. He thinks I'm obsessed with males, but I assure you I hate every male that exists on earth and wish they were never born to begin with. Except you of course.

Should I have played innocent when I returned home after hearing the news? Should I have begged Mother to recall her statement and inform the school that everything Father claimed to have seen was false?
Should I have knocked on his gate, instead of pacing back and forth before I left after seeing a car honk and head in?
Should I have dashed in together with the car and beg for his hand in marriage while on my knees? Yelled at Mother when she inquired for the truth after I came back from school?
Should I have reassured his parents that I desired to be with their son for the rest of my life?

Should I have thrown my hesitations down the bin and done all of it?

Even right now I haven't the slightest idea what it is I should do. I feel conflicted.

I feel different.
It feels like I'm not the person I think I am, and it scares me.

I cherish consistence and ever since I met him, I've been nothing but inconsistent. Is it for the best I'm now rid of him?

Father asked for him to be expelled and his record doesn't bode well for him. I'm worried, but his brother refuses to update me. It's been two weeks.

Should I leave for his house again, will I be able to do it this time? I have no idea how he's faring. Is he getting beaten, I'll take the hits in his stead.
Is he disappointed in me?

I just messaged his brother, but he left me on read. What to do? What to do?

I'm in a state of panic but all I can do is wait until I can see him by chance. But if I do see him, what happens then?

A WALK IN THE RAIN

Should I hug him and ask him how he's faring?
Will he push me away, thinking everything was my fault to begin with.

I hope it's the latter.

He got expelled. His brother replied.
There is only one person to blame, and it's Father.

Once again, you were right, and I was wrong.

I hate him so much.
I hate him, I hate him, I hate him, I hate him....

TILL NEXT TIME OR NOT

MEMORY: OUR FAULTS

After finishing the JAMB (Joint Admissions and Matriculation Board), Father signed her up for a week practice course in Ife in preparations for her post-UTME. It was recommended by a renowned teacher, so Father immediately accepted.

He wasn't to return until later that year, so he left the preparations to Mother. She drove her to the location, packed some necessities and gave her pocket money.
She had a mattress, an emergency stove, a bucket, bathroom essentials, clothes and more.

The dorm was 10 minutes away from the school, by car. It was fairly decent.

A week after, the examination day came.
Nonchalant she answered the questions and left as soon as she was done.

An hour later, she got a call.
Father ordered to return home that same day. Mother was out on a competition with her team and was to return later that evening; it was impossible to pick her up. But Father's orders remained unchanged, so Mother asked an acquaintance for help.

30. sept. 20:18. He came. It was a familiar face.

Hands full with her luggage, they left for the garage. Father's order meant they had to use public transport.

The conductor overcharged them for two seats. The cash the man had in hand wasn't enough, so Debbie offered her unspent pocket money, but he refused. He said it was no bother for him to carry her on his legs. Although he might have been unbothered, she wasn't. Tired, she left him alone.

...

Maybe that was the starting point of the turning point. If that is the case, then Father is the one to blame.

...

1st Oct. 2019.
Time passed, and they safely arrived home.

It's Independence Day.
Debbie's first thought after she heard the bark of her one-year-old puppy.

"Thank God you arrived home safely".

Mother opened the gate, hugged her daughter and thanked the man, asking him to sleep the night over; it was too late.

Hearing these words, Debbie muttered her discontent towards Father. Mother helped with the mattress and the rest were easy to carry. To avoid waking Wande and the youngest, they left the organising till dawn.

Mother tired of staying up late, retired to her room and Debbie tired, for an entirely different reason, turned on the TV. It was an unfamiliar channel, but she left it there. The moving images and faint voices sufficed.

The man took a mattress from the passage and laid it on the floor in the living room. Done with his preparations, he turned off the TV and asked her to retire for the night. "You need to sleep, it's quite late", he said.

She left for the room. Her siblings were there.

Unable to sleep, she returned to the living room and asked if she could watch the TV until she slept off. He hesitated for a while before finally giving in. He turned off the lights, making the Christmas lights more visible, cozied himself up, tossed a little and said: happy new month.

Two to three hours passed before fatigue found its way to her. Till then she blankly stared at the TV, drank a cup of water when her throat felt dry before returning to the sofa again, repeating the same thing all over, until she closed her eyes and fell asleep on the sofa.

Tic. Toc. Tic. Toc.

When she woke up, she was on the bed. It felt like only three minutes had passed and the sky was still dark. Upon opening her eyes, an ominous feeling crept in and so did a mixture of fear and horror.

Properly taking in the situation, she made eye contact with the culprit. Her eyes welled up, his pleaded for mercy.

30-10-2019

I'm crying, you're wet; drenched in tears of my disgrace.

What to do? What to do?
I'm with child.

I've thought it through several times, and I think the best option is to stab him, when I see him.

I've picked up the knife several times only to drop it back. I don't know what is stopping me, but whatever it is I want to get rid of it.
I want it out, but I don't know how to.

I'm surprised by the fact that what I fear isn't Mother and Father finding out, it's the life growing inside me coming out.

I have found myself constantly touching my belly, boring my nails into it, thinking:
It must not be born.

I am too imperfect for it.
The world is too imperfect for it.

Whenever I saw homeless mothers and children on the street, I sometimes gave them money but most of the time I turned away.

Never would I have imagined myself releasing a kid into this world of imperfection, to birth a life into one I wish I wasn't in.

A WALK IN THE RAIN

I puked at the thought of procreating.
I spat at the idea of having another like me.
I shuddered at the image of Father having a grandchild.

...

Just yesterday, I asked a friend of mine to help me purchase rat poison. I couldn't take the risk of buying it myself. This estate is too small.
He might come with it tomorrow, that is, if Mother leaves early for work.

I hope I have the heart to consume it.
I hope it kills me too.

I'm speechless.
Was I drugged? I have no idea.

My memory's fuzzy but it felt like I was asleep for only a minute or two.

I regret having not stabbed him upon waking up. I hate seeing him visit our house freely, while I ponder on what to do with my life, on what to do with the contempt.

Maybe if that never happened, I could have lived just a little bit longer till death found its way to me. But there's no time. I have to do it now no matter the cost, no matter the suffering of a lifetime. Yankee what would you have me do?

Mother has been paying me too much attention lately. She says I look different and wants to take me to the hospital for a check-up.

Since the incident, before realising I hadn't seen my period and before the shameless man asked me to take a pregnancy test, I've been drinking whatever I could find. From Lipton tea bags, to chlorine, to hypo. Everything I knew and heard to be unhealthy, I consumed. Everyone around me says I'm growing lean but I'm yet to see it. The life in me has managed to survive this long and so have I. It's taking too much time and Mother's growing suspicious.

Last week Tuesday, Mother took me for a check-up, which was obviously a lie. Upon getting there, the nurses played along with Mother's lie and told me to give them a urine sample, they said they wanted to check if there were signs of infection. Only a fool would fall for that.

As sample, I scooped the water from their toilet and thankfully, it was dirty enough to convince them. I thought if Mother found out, things would become bothersome. She'd cry, tell our relatives. They too will in turn cry, yell, blame me, look at me with either pity or contempt. I don't even want to imagine how ugly things could have turned out.

In 9 days, I'm to turn 16. Father turned up for the last two previous celebrations and stayed a while, however, this year will be a little bit different.

A WALK IN THE RAIN

Even though Mother and Father played smart by keeping us in the dark for a while, I had long since known about the move to Father – a few weeks after we travelled to Abuja for our passports.

It's been months since we went to Abuja and got our passports. At first, I thought nothing of it, since they needed to be renewed anyway after our last application to travel to Italy 5 or 7 years ago. A trip that never came to be, because it wasn't an appropriate place to raise a kid and we weren't old enough to grow up in an entirely new different society, at least that's what Father said. According to Mother, Father thinks where he now resides is far much better than any of the countries he has been in.

This new utopia of his is probably also in Europe, but I have no idea where. Wande does, but I don't want to ask her, since I wouldn't make it till then anyway. It makes me almost regret not having given the nurses and Mother what they wanted.

The plan is to, after my birthday, take us all with him.

To fasten the process, I need the rat poison tomorrow and I have a good feeling about this; it finally feels like this will be my final input here.

When the sun rises, I will be burning you dear diary. I cannot afford to have you disclose too much. You, a collection of memories not even Mother and Father know of.

While I disclose things about me to you, I never confided in you. I merely left behind traces to look back upon during my last moments, last hours, last days, or last months and now feels like the time. So since you know too much, you must be burnt. Harsh? No.

While it might take a while to burn all your pages, it took me seconds to discard all that has been. With that said, I say adjö to you, the only one that knows my secrets.

Goodbye.

MEMORY: 8.11.2019

The poison is slowly killing me. Father says I'm lean.
Maybe soon, I'll be dead.
I'm excited.

For 6 days, I've consumed the rat poison, one before and after every meal. Just this morning, after Father prayed for me as a birthday ritual, I consumed three packets at once. My throat felt extra dry.

Everyone but me is busy with the preparations, so I'm left alone on the bed in our room. Since I just ate breakfast, I think it's okay to take two more.
I want to and I have to.

Father says we will be leaving on the 14th. That's too soon. I need more, but I only have 15 left – 3 for 5 days – and there are six days left. I wonder what will happen if I were to consume all 15 now. Should I? I want to.

I have taken two extra, and, for the third time today, just brushed my teeth. I can't be too careful...

...

Wande just came in to call me, the guests are arriving.

I'm all dressed up. Father was right after all, I **am** lean. The gown feels out of place compared to when we bought it. Although not many will notice since I've been indoors since my post-UTME examination, my family would. But regardless I'm happy, it's a sign of my progress.

Soon they won't have to spend money to buy a sheep, hire cooks, prepare a feast, invite visitors for a child that couldn't care less.

Soon I won't have to smile at strangers and thank them for attending my party, thank them for their generous presents and witness another day like today.

Soon I'll be free of the burden of living in fear of what tomorrow holds. Soon I'll be free of the burden of forever living with him till the day he allows me my independence either through marriage or work.

Soon I'll be where I belong.
I'm excited.

A WALK IN THE RAIN

November 2019

This is how it ends.

Your fear of pain has pushed things long enough. We know your limit. You have not only reached it, but you've also passed it, let us handle the rest. Sleep. It will be over before you know it.

Did you know that your fears aside you have always rebuked our prayers for us. While we beg one thing, you wish for another. We'll say something and you'll say something else.

Unus pro-omnibus, omnes pro uno.
We are forever one; bound together by fate and experience we will never abandon you. Others might, but we never will. We have long since supported your actions and we hope you do ours. To defeat our common enemy, we need you onboard with this decision.

Look around you.
Father's is the toilet, and the others are asleep. The window to your left, two seats' forwards, is open. Your chance of succeeding is almost a hundred percent.

All you've done since you got onboard is listen to depressing songs, what more do you need to convince you of our resolve. You've done what you wanted, you've cried, you've bawled, you've let out all you thought it was that held you back.

A WALK IN THE RAIN

You know, just as well as we do, that your chances of surviving is less than zero.

For the first time since your birthday death feels so near, we can smell it. All you have to do to embrace it is to get up. Put your letter to Father in your bag so your family sees it afterwards. Leave your socks on, push your way out of your row if you have to but approach your target like a ghost.

You have a maximum of ten seconds. Harden your resolve now before it's too late. We promise to be with you through it all. Together, we'll take the leap towards our future, but without you, there's nothing we can do.

While we can sense your hesitation and worries, we think of them as nothing but excuses. The couple sleeping right beside the window is none of your concern, their life after you shouldn't concern you.

Which do you prefer?
They being bothered by nightmares for a year or two, or you living with Father every minute and every second of your life till you either get a job he desires, or marry a man he consents of, a man you will one day procreate with. Worth remembering is that in you is another life, one that must never see the light as you.

While you might think Father would kill you upon finding out, we know from experience that it's all wishful thinking.

8 months isn't enough time, it's too little.
It is either now or never.
Jump. Jump. Jump. Jump.

*Jump. Jump. Jump. Jump.
Jump. Jump. Jump. Jump.
Jum...*

*It's the best decision you'll ever make. So, JUMP
JUMP*

A WALK IN THE RAIN

DEAR FATHER

A WALK IN THE RAIN

Hi there Father.
You're probably wondering why I wrote this but don't be too worried, you're about to find out.

First the good news. I'm sure that by the time you're reading this I'll be long gone. I'll be in a place you cannot find me, as long as you're alive that is. More importantly, I died killing something I'm happy never got to see you.

There were times I wanted to yell out the depths of my heart to you, but I persevered. I knew the repercussions. All my life I've been patient for this moment and I'm happy it finally came. I'm happy I no longer have to see your face, withstand your hypocrisy, tolerate your obstinacy, revere you like you were a god.

In this life, there were two things I couldn't tolerate. You and Life. You know what I told myself?
"Father is life and life is Father".

I've long since known where it was I was headed, and while I knew what that meant, I accepted it.

But did you know, Father. Did you ever foresee this. I'm curious if you ever saw it coming. While you planned, so did I. while you built your image of me, I did too. The only difference was I looked at what I had in front of me, you didn't.

I always knew that I might not live long enough to show you just how much hate I have accumulated for you over time, to show you the extent of hate I harbour towards you. I, already at 10, knew I might not live to see the day when you cry, regretting your life decisions and actions. But at the same time, I'm cherishing this moment, the moment I get to reveal all this to you.

Oh Father, you have no idea. You have no idea how much I want you to realise your very life principal is what makes me hate you so. I wish there is a life after this and another after that. Lives where you get to live the life I have lived.

I wish there is someone that will see to it that you experience double the pain I feel, experience triple the injustice.

These are all the things I wanted to say to your face Father, but what would you have done if you had gotten to hear this all those years ago. the first time I wrote down in my heart.

Would you have punished me? Would you have pretended to understand me only to later use that as an excuse to justify your accusations against mother for her "poor conduct and lack of attention towards the kids"? Or would you genuinely have assured me you'd change? Or do you, like I believe you probably do now as you are reading this, believe your ways are just and always have been?

Hmmm, Father. What would you have done?
And if you act like I have predicted, who should I blame?

Should I blame the old ways for making you this way?
Should I blame the time you grew up in, or the patriarchal society you were raised in that places you above everyone else, Mother, your kids, your peers both male and female alike?
Should I blame your individual way of thinking that you are always right except those few times you openly acknowledge small mistakes in front of us.

Things I couldn't ask you, at least not until now.

Before picking this pen up I felt suffocated, my thoughts were chaotic and my mind was turbulent. But now it's all blank.

I'm telling myself to let my emotions write, but that's not what I want. What I wish to convey is something more articulated than mere feelings. I wish to convey to you, words that have hidden themselves within my unconsciousness and are at the moment holding me back from wishing you well, from thanking you for your fatherly efforts – by your definition. Words holding me back from leaving without shedding a tear.

I wish to convey to you much more...

Hatred.
Father.

You see, these two words are the only two consistent things in my heart, mind, and soul as of now. And because they've been roaming around for a while now, I decided to write them down. However, it's worth noting that after writing them down, neither of them make me feel anything as they once did.

Whenever I saw you come back from your trip, take out those new, fancy, western clothes you never failed to bring with you for my sister and I, I crumbled. I silently begged for you to stop. Your gestures of good will bore great weight, they weighed down heavily and my resolve and often destroyed the bricks of hatred I so carefully constructed in your absence.

I thought it unfair that only I was subjected to such. I would be the one to be flogged for trivial things, and at the same time the one expected to love the flogger. To appreciate their efforts and understand them. I was always the one that had to heed a hypocrite with my heads down, as the hypocrite taught me to adhere to principles they never once lived by.

You, Father, were to me the embodiment of disgrace, shame, hypocrisy, obstinacy, and many more.

Despite this, I let it all go while reminding myself of the great efforts Mother claims you put into your gifts and other monetary involvement in our lives. Too much of the same routine and I grew to understand that I could thank you for all this without respecting you as a father, as my dad.
I grew to understand that you had, in fact, done nothing to deserve being called daddy by anyone – in an affectionate manner.

The only thing I can then conclude my gratitude with is your effort in paying our school fees, building us a house, getting me Yankee. Although you separated us, I guess I could still thank you for giving her to me in the first place.

Now, back to the person who must have initially found this letter, I also have my thanks to give.

I thank Mother for reminding me that Father was suffering for us.
I thank mother for resorting to words to chastise me.
I thank mother for leaving me in the hands of those who took advantage of my young age and innocence.
I thank mother for her continuous efforts to be emotionally and financially available.

To you both, I thank your absence Father and Mother's opposite nature, when compared to you.

Worth mentioning Father, are the things I have come to understand thanks to you – or rather thanks to my observations.

It does not suffice to only learn from experience, adapting what is learnt to what is in front of me matters more than just releasing my load.
You made me think twice of what it means to really care for someone and to claim to care for someone.
One-sidedly expressing what I claim to be care and carefully observing what it is I want to care for, before expressing my care, are ultimately polar opposites as we are.

There were times I couldn't help but share this opinion with you; but I'm but a dumb kid, what could I possibly know.
You claim I'm intelligent but disregard my opinions saying it's

a kid talking, oblivious of the kid's very best. It made me wonder just when I will stop being a kid to you. when you will grow past thinking it's a kid talking, and most importantly is when you will stop thinking everything I do, by default, means I'm rebelling against my parents – 'because I've reached that age'...

Thanks to you I have come to realise the reality of what I once thought of as my predicament.
There is no use crying over spilled milk – what has opened has happened, the only thing I can change or influence is what comes after.
Trust no one – all males want one thing and I must protect my body, mind and soul from them, excluding family.
My status as a child is no different from a slave's and I am nothing but an investment,
Being older does not mean I'm all that it, in fact it means whatever I say is the teenager in me acting up.
Respect is to be earned regardless of status, your title as my father never meant you knew better or deserved better and your actions tell me you are not worthy of my respect.
Being raped or molested does not mean it's the end of the world. Afterall, there are others out there without shelter, starving, homeless living every day without knowing what tomorrow holds.

Father I could go on and on as to how much I have come to understand from observing you, but I'd rather make you understand why I never thought good of you. Why the emotions I feel towards you are nothing but negative, and the words I have to describe you contradicts Mother's, yours, our family friends' and even Wande's.

Not once have you thought of your irrelevant display of authority and your so-called disciplinarian actions as unnecessary.
Like when Wande made a mistake and dropped your laptop bag, you responded with a slap.

She was barely five.
She might have forgotten, but I never will.

Every time I had to receive a punishment for another hostellite's wrongdoing or inefficiency. I thought of you Father.
Each time I got flogged for being a second late to the refectory, chapel, or any gathering with hell canes. I thought of Father.
Every time I got threatened that I would be publicly shamed for being a bed wetter, I thought of you. Before I knew it the anger in me was getting wild and wanted to do terrible things that has already become a part of me.
We started planning, the plans were simple but mischievous – I would stand back and watch you destroy everything, all it is you claim to have worked hard for, including your greatest investment ever.

M E.

This conniving part of me, I grew to love.
It helped not only calm the anger I could no longer control, but

to also throw away the last bit of empathy I had for you. I was grateful to it; I could finally breathe.

Father did you know it's easier to destroy than to build.
I remember most of my childhood being spent building a fortress. I wanted a fortress strong enough to withstand the persuasions, pity, empathy, child-like love and appreciation your monetary endeavours brought with them. And I'm glad to inform you that I have succeeded in shielding my heart and mind from being confused and transformed by you, from being persuaded.

Mother says you work really hard to pay our tuition fees and that it shows how much you love us. Somehow, I managed to get fooled every time, that is until you visited.

Whenever you visited, I found myself studying you.
I, with time, came to realise that hidden beneath your fancy perfume was the stench of exhaustion.

A sign that the slightest mistake could tick you off.

Whenever I saw how much mechanical repair you had to do on your visits that were supposed to be your vacation, I felt bad. I felt bad for refusing the life you had worked so hard to create for me and convinced myself to bear with whatever inconveniencies I might have. I utilised your efforts and mustered up courage to keep my mouth shut and close my eyes whenever those consistent molesting hands of my 'uncles' tore down my innocence as a girl – I didn't want to worry mother, she had to work. I couldn't tell you; you had a heavier cross to bear.

But those resolves never lasted a year,
because you visited every year.

Not one of your visits went by without you yelling, shouting, complaining, and hitting when things slightly deviate from what you'd consider proper behaviour, womanly duties, and filial obligations.

At 10 I got tired; I was tired of your flimsy attitude. Why was it always you that had to be held with care?
Why did Mother always tell us to understand your situation...and why did we have to listen when you never tried?
Why does it seem like I'm the parent and not you?

I have always told myself to not care, to remain unbothered. But I know deep down, that if I ever manage to survive and live long enough to build myself back up, I will repay you for the efforts you put in my life both financially and emotionally and I will make sure to pay you back 10 folds.

Even though, to me, this is nothing but a repetition, something I have been telling myself since the teeth incident that you probably don't remember.
I'm glad it's news to you.

At one point I even thought it was all my fault, that I was the naughty one to have been punished every time you visited but that wasn't the case, Father. I doubt you ever thought through

why none of your visits went by without you hitting me.
Was calling Wande a snake out of annoyance worse than breaking the smartphone you bought out of frustration that I got a lighter punishment for the latter? I never understood the logic.

I have revisited my memories over and over and I am convinced of my resolve...

If I'm to spend every single day of my life with you, I cannot think of a better way than this. I'd rather put an end to it all, that wait for you to not only find out about the life in me but drive me to insanity.

Father, did you know love kills; it scars.
With just a loss, love could make you think and do unimaginable things, at least for me.

Upon my first return home, I got to know that we had moved from the house that holds all traces of our history. As if that wasn't enough, I heard Yankee disappeared three months before my arrival. Three months!!! And no one bothered to inform me.

Yankee's disappearance and possible death was a consequence of Mother's and Wande's laziness, lack of attention and most importantly the cruelty of humans.

A WALK IN THE RAIN

As young as most claim me to be,
I know better than to not check if the dog is where I last saw her after shutting the gates. I know better than to go out without kissing my dog goodbye. I know better than to take a knife and kill a family member out of spite.

Hatred is what I felt after hearing the news of Yankee's disappearance, it was directed not only at my reckless sister and Mother but also at our neighbours.
It was childish; throwing a stone at a domesticated dog.

Oh, how the tables would have turned if I had a gun.

Humans can be so cruel and despite their attempts, I refuse to belong to the cruellest of them all. I found it hard to understand that the very same people that went to our house every time you threw me a birthday party, the same lowlifes that accepted those birthday presents dared raise their hands to stone a dog, my dog.

Cheapskates, lowlifes, hypocrites, it doesn't suffice to curse them out. They took the only one thing that gave me joy and made life bearable. You took me away from her.

Seven years.
Yankee and I had spent seven years together and she knew everything about me as I did her. Remembering being the last to hear of her certain demise hurts. Her disappearance left me lonely; it left me with no one to lie beside during hard times, no one to watch the moon with, no one to love. But while I do

regret her death I refused to live for revenge and I'm sure Yankee understands why.

Afterall, I'm different from you, and that will forever remain the case.

You act on fear more than anything.
You fear things would go awry and act thinking that what you do would end up being for the best, but the fact is that it isn't.

You are by many factors, mostly your surroundings convinced into thinking your actions as an adult, a father and a husband would ultimately be for the best, but I'm sorry to break this to you Father, it isn't.

When you fail to see what is in front of you and act on what you believe to be in front of you, then it is not wonder that things play out differently. It is no wonder, that the situation spirals and goes out of hand. It is no wonder that nothing could ever manage to repair the distance between us.

If reincarnation does exist, I hope we, Yankee and I, could be reborn as parents of each other in all our lifetimes. I also hope we, that is you and I, get reborn as counterparts of each other in our next life – a life where I have the upper hand.

Even now I'm doubtful.
There were times I questioned myself. What if that feeling was right all along. What if all of this is just a pretence? What if I am a pretence. What if the very foundation of who I think I

have grown to be was all based on pretence – and I in fact want to live?

Do you perhaps know the answer, dear Father?

A. WALK. IN. THE. RAIN

POEM

I breathe and I have organs,
I bleed so I have blood.
I think I have my own thoughts.
I am bred so I have my own parents
What am I?

I'm human.

I'm endowed with scars from earlier efforts to be set free.
The direction we are headed is the only gleam of hope I have left.

Death.

I'm greedy,
I desire to shorten the trip to our certain end, to my certain end.
Small and young as I am,
I'm unable to accomplish a thing of desire
I can only think dream, and hope.

I'm crazy,
I have voices in my head telling me how to live
I love them and want them to stay.
They keep me sane.

Ironic much.

A WALK IN THE RAIN

I'm forced by many factors to have no say in my birth, my death.
The decision on whether to live or die lies on those who own one,
My hands are tied as I'm dragged through the market - my passage of time
Bound to my owners I await the day the chains break.

Thanks A.D.A.

Copyright © 2024.
The author reserves all rights to be recognized as the owner of this work. You may not sell or reproduce any part of this book without written consent from the copyright owner.

First hardcover edition February 2024.
Book design by Debbie Walters, also known as, Debbie Ade.
ISBN 978-91-527-9633-7 (paperback edition)
Printed and bound by Amazon.

All rights reserved, including the right to reproduce this book or portions thereof in any form whatsoever. For information, address the author on her official website: www.debbie-ada-walters.com

Printed in Poland
by Amazon Fulfillment
Poland Sp. z o.o., Wrocław

35742243R00142